SPOOKED SOLID

MYSTIC INN MYSTERIES

STEPHANIE DAMORE

PINK SAPPHIRE PRESS

ONE

"Two more bats, and I think that'll do it," I said out loud to myself while putting the finishing touches on the bookstore's decorations. My friend and store's owner, Misty, had decided to host a Halloween party at the bookstore tonight, complete with costumes and spooky stories. Unfortunately, or maybe it should be fortunately, the store was swamped lately, and Misty hadn't had the time to decorate. That's where I stepped in, spending the day stringing glittery orange garland around the crown molding, blowing up purple and green balloons, and strategically hanging sparkling sequin bats from the ceiling. I leaned back from the top of the ladder to admire my work. It wasn't bad. Maybe one more bat. I bent forward, grabbing another sequined decoration from the ladder's shelf.

"Mew?" The cat's questioning chirp caught my attention.

I looked down at the black cat standing under my open ladder.

"Where did you come from?" I asked while tacking a piece of tape to the bat's string and hanging it on the door frame. The bat dangled the perfect height just above the front door.

"Is your owner nearby?" I looked down at the cat who stared up quizzically at the decoration as if she'd love nothing more than to swat at it.

The cat didn't reply, and honestly, it could've gone either way. Living in an enchanted town, you never knew what to expect. I should know. I felt the weight of the tiger eye on my chest—a magical necklace and family heirloom that granted me the power to transform into a feline myself.

"You know, it's bad luck having a black cat under a ladder-like that," Misty hollered over to me after ringing up a customer and wishing them a happy Halloween.

"Hush now. Like this adorable creature would curse me." No sooner were the words out of my mouth did Aunt Thelma rush in the door and bang right into the ladder. The force of her impact rocked the ladder away from me, and I pitched forward, clinging precariously to the doorframe. The ladder toppled, crashing into the front book display and tipping over a decorative, bubbling cauldron in the process. Water spilled onto the floor and sent the cat scurrying with a disapproving yowl.

"Save the books!" Misty shouted, grabbing a roll of paper towels from under the counter and racing forward. I dropped down from the doorframe, thankful I was dangling only a few feet off the ground. Together, we sopped up as much water as possible while Aunt Thelma righted the ladder and used her shawl to wipe off the book jackets. Misty ran to the back storage room and came back waving hand towels. We worked to dry everything thoroughly. Thankful that the floor took most of the water.

Aunt Thelma touched my arm and opened her mouth as if to ask, "Are you alright?" But instead, she croaked out a "RIBBIT?"

Her hand flew up to her throat. Aunt Thelma coughed and shook her head.

"What was that?" I asked.

"RIBBIT. JUG-O-RUM. CROAK," Aunt Thelma tried again.

"What in the world?" Misty paused with her arms full of damp towels. She stood off to the side, listening to Aunt Thelma and what sounded like a string of frog expletives.

"RIBBIT! PLUNK! JUG-O-RUM!" The sounds punctuated the air. Aunt Thelma's eyes were wide, and her arms flailed around with each attempt.

I touched my aunt's arm and leaned forward,

hoping my touch would calm her. "Have you been spelled?"

Aunt Thelma held up her hands as if to say she didn't know. Shopping bags from the Village Center shops slid down from her wrists to her elbows. Aunt Thelma had been all over the outdoor shopping district and had returned with purchases from the bakery, candle store, and the yarn shop from the looks of it.

"Well, if it's a spell, that should be an easy fix," Misty looked to me to reverse the spell, but I wasn't about to try. The last time someone spelled someone in the bookstore, it hadn't ended well. Plus, half the time, my spells ended in disaster anyway. I didn't need to turn Aunt Thelma permanently into a frog.

Sensing my hesitation, Misty dropped the towels, pulled out her wand and aimed it at my aunt's chest.

I squeezed my eyes shut, not wanting to watch in case things went awry.

Misty cleared her throat and proclaimed the general counterspell, "Tixie!"

A small whoosh of air sailed toward Aunt Thelma, but that was all I heard. No gasps, shrieks of panic or general chaos—for once. Slowly, I opened one eye and then the other.

Aunt Thelma stood before me, looking the same as ever.

"Well?" Misty asked my aunt. Her wand was in her fisted hand on her hip.

Aunt Thelma opened her mouth to speak.

I crossed my fingers.

"RIBBIT." The deep baritone sound rolled off her tongue.

Aunt Thelma's shoulders dropped.

My heart sank. "What does that mean?" I asked the duo.

"I don't know. It could be a curse." Misty's brow furrowed in concentration.

A line was forming at the register again, and an employee called to Misty.

"I'll be back as soon as I can," Misty said before turning and leaving.

I looked to my aunt. "How long have you been croaking for?"

Aunt Thelma held up a finger in response.

"One day?" I guessed. I hadn't seen my aunt this morning at the inn she owned, and I managed, so I supposed it was possible she had woken up this way.

She shook her head no.

"One hour?" I tried again.

Aunt Thelma huffed and walked over to the register, where Misty supplied her with a pen and paper.

I trailed after her.

Aunt Thelma scribbled a reply. "Just now!" was her response, followed with, "I'm going to the tea shop."

"Good idea. Clemmie will know what to do." My

aunt's best friend sold plenty of herbal remedies at her store, Sit For A Spell. Maybe she had one for frog curses. If not, I was sure she'd know how to fix it or who to call.

"Good luck. I'll check in with you in a bit." I offered a tight-lipped smile.

Aunt Thelma left with a nod and a croak. I watched her walk out the door and hoped Clemmie really would know what to do.

"Did you say curse? What do you know about them?" Percy, Mystic Inn's resident poltergeist, whispered in my ear. His cold breath caught me by surprise.

I slapped my hand on my heart. "Geez, Percy, you have to quit doing that." I took a moment for my heart to steady and take in the ghost's transparent form. "What are you doing here?" I rubbed my chest with the heel of my hand. Percy's random pop-ups were honestly giving me chest pains. I was convinced he'd be the death of me yet.

Percy wasn't paying attention to me. He'd floated over to a bookcase and was scanning the spines. His eyes trailed up and down as he read the vertical titles.

I walked towards him. "What is up with you?" First, Percy started dressing up in bow ties and sport coats, and now he was spending more and more time away from the inn. In fact, I'd never even seen him at the bookstore before. Usually, he only scared the daylights out of me at the inn.

Percy ignored my question. "I need to find out about curses, and fast. What do you know?" Percy rounded on me. The poltergeist's eyes bore into mine.

I leaned back, looking at Percy as if I could see right through to his brain like I could the rest of him. But whatever Percy was thinking, he wasn't willing to share it.

"C'mon, Jelly. I don't have time." Percy looked pained.

"Percy, what's going on? Are you okay?" I reached forward as if I could lay my hand on his arm to comfort him.

"Oh, never mind. I'll ask someone else." Percy huffed and disappeared in a blink of an eye, leaving me standing there befuddled.

"Well, okay then." I darted my eyes from side to side and wondered if anyone else, like Misty, had witnessed Percy's odd behavior.

But Misty's attentions were elsewhere, and everyone else seemed lost in a good book or their own worlds.

I blew out a sigh and wondered why Percy was researching curses, and then I thought of Aunt Thelma and wondered if the two incidents were somehow related. As much as I wanted to dismiss it, I couldn't deny the uneasiness that began to creep through my veins and settle into my bones. Had Percy somehow managed to curse Aunt Thelma?

Percy was mischievous, but he'd never messed with Aunt Thelma a day in his afterlife. But maybe he knew who had? That was more likely, but for the life of me, I couldn't think of who would do such a thing. One thing was certain, not all was what it seemed to be in my sleepy, little, enchanted town.

I'd bet my wand on it.

Not that I could do anything about it. Not right now. We had a party to prepare for.

I shifted my focus to the Halloween decorations, taking in my work, and admitting everything looked great. Even with the water fiasco, Spellbinding Books looked perfect. The decorations were sparkly and spooky. The perfect combination for a family-friendly party.

With that job checked off my list, and believe me, it had been a job, I decided it was time to step outside and fetch my costume from the shop around the corner. I'd requested a dark red velvet cloak and wicker handbasket to portray my favorite childhood spooky story, Little Red Riding Hood. The costume seemed spot-on for a Halloween party at a bookstore, or at least I thought it was until I saw Misty's regency ball gown. My best friend decided to pay homage to Elizabeth Bennet from Pride and Preju-dice. With her high-waisted gown with its squared neckline, puffed sleeves, and lace skirt, Misty looked like she stepped right off the pages of the regency romance.

I blinked a time or two as I took in her appearance. "You look stunning."

"This old thing?" Misty joked as she picked at the invisible lint on her shoulder. "Think Mr. Darcy will like it?"

"If he's anything like Peter, I'm sure he will," I said with a wink. Peter was the owner of the wand shop, Sticks, and the man Misty was currently dating.

"Let's hope so. I have no idea how women wore dresses like this every day." Misty adjusted the neckline..

"Me either, girl. Me either."

Misty moved over to the counter where her white satin gloves were, and I watched as she slid them up to her elbows.

"Speaking of costumes, I need to go pick up mine. I'll be back in a minute. Not looking as fabulous as you, mind you, but back nonetheless," I announced.

"Hush now. I'm sure your cloak will be adorable."

"Just what every woman wants to hear," I joked as I waved goodbye to Misty and slipped out the front door before she could reply.

Outside, the sun was setting, streaking the sky in purples and oranges. The air had a slight nip to it, a refreshing change after the scorching sun-kissed days that had lingered in the south. Every time I thought the heat was gone for good, it came back with a vengeance, summer refusing to concede to fall.

I looked around at the youngest trick-or-treaters starting to arrive and smiled broadly. Halloween in Silverlake truly was the most magical time of the year. Mortals could have Christmas. I'd take candy, costumes, and magic any day. Sorry, Santa.

When I was little, and my mom was alive, she'd make the most intricate Halloween costumes for me. Whether it was a beautiful butterfly with metallic wings or the pumpkin princess gown she'd stitched together with silver thread that shimmered under the full moon, I always felt like the queen of Halloween when I stepped outside to collect my candy.

Now that I was an adult, I realized how much love went into making each costume, and it was that love that made them so special. What made *me* feel so special when I wore them.

My mind was lost in thought, taking a bittersweet trip down memory lane when I rounded the corner and came up short.

Vance was walking straight towards me.

Many might think I'd be happy to see my former ex-boyfriend and newly established friend, but they didn't know what happened during the final night of the fall festival, and right at that moment, I didn't have the mental facilities to explain it.

Like a deer in headlights, I froze. Finally, I found

my feet and darted abruptly into the nearest shop, which happened to be Mix it Up!, the potions shop.

I must've looked wild because Connie, the shop's proprietor, raced forward.

"Is everything all right?" She placed a steadying hand on my arm and searched my face.

"What?" I snuck a glance over my shoulder to make sure Vance hadn't spotted me. A few of the youngest trick-or-treaters had started arriving. He'd stopped to talk with a young family. I stared, watching the friendly exchange.

I realized a moment later that Connie was still standing there, waiting for an explanation.

"Oh, um..." I stammered as my mind raced to come up with an excuse for my erratic behavior.

Connie raised her eyebrows.

I cleared my throat. "I'm fine, really. Just scared myself."

Connie looked over my shoulder out the window. I followed her gaze. Vance waved goodbye to the ballerina and dinosaur-costumed toddlers, smiling at the parents as he continued his way down the path.

"I see." The corner of Connie's mouth twitched into a smile.

I shrank back from the window, wishing a hole would open up and swallow me.

But a hole didn't magically appear, and Connie was too polite to pry. Thank the universe for small favors.

"I don't suppose I can interest you in a calming potion...or a love potion," Connie added with a sly smile.

Or perhaps she wasn't.

I was sure I blushed from the tip of my nose right down to my toes. "No, I'm fine, but thank you." I took two full steps inside the shop, putting as much distance between Vance and me as possible. The wall of cauldrons to the right caught my eye. Aunt Thelma owned a cauldron, but I'd never had a need for one of my own. Perhaps it was time I changed that. I was no longer a reluctant witch. And sure, my spells might go awry more often than not, but maybe I'd have better luck with potions? It was worth a shot.

"What about these cauldrons? What should a beginner look for?" I stepped closer to the towering wall. Connie had recently expanded her stock, and it had already been impressive before. Now, in addition to the various sizes, Connie also offered a selection of materials.

"Is that copper?"

"It is, but those work best for burning herbs or incense, not potions. The metal can contaminate the liquid." Connie stared at me for a moment, her fingertip thoughtfully tapping her lips. "I assume it's potions you're looking at working with?"

I nodded.

"Then I'd say this one would be best."

Connie stepped forward and pulled a medium-sized cauldron from the shelf, holding it out to me by the arching metal handle. The cast-iron piece was the size of a large stockpot with three angled pegs for legs. I took the cauldron from Connie and examined it closely, having no idea really what I was looking for. The cauldron was sturdy and plenty big enough.

"The legs were cast at the same time as the rest of the pot," Connie explained, flipping the pot over in my hand. "So, you won't have to worry about leaks. The riveted ones always leak."

I nodded again, having never thought of such a thing.

"Just give it a good seasoning like you'd do a new cast-iron skillet and you're good to go."

"Oil and salt?"

"Yes, ma'am. That's the way."

"Okay, I'll take it then."

"Excellent. I'll throw in my book to get you started too."

Connie had recently published a potions cookbook. I'd glanced at it a couple times at Misty's bookshop but hadn't had a chance to really dive into it.

"That would be wonderful."

Connie rang me up, and I reminded myself that I really must be on my way, that is until Connie asked if there was anything else she could help me with. I thought of Aunt Thelma and remembered Percy's odd behavior. "You don't, by chance, know anything about frog curses, do you?"

"Talk to me about it."

"Well, Aunt Thelma was at the bookstore a bit ago, and she randomly started croaking. She doesn't have a clue how it started, and Misty tried a counter-spell, but...," I shrugged my shoulders to say that it hadn't worked.

"Hmm. Curses can be tricky. Do you know if she bought any new jewelry recently?"

"I'm not sure." Instinctively, I rubbed the tiger's eye between my thumb and forefinger.

Connie caught the motion and smiled.

I dropped my amulet. "She had a few shopping bags with her, I guess I can ask her."

"I'd suggest you start there. Curses and jewels go hand in hand. Actually, any knickknack or small arti-fact. Maybe she picked something up today."

"Good idea, thanks."

"In the meantime, let me know if you change your mind about that love potion. I can have Vance eating out of the palm of your hand in seconds."

I stumbled over my words, trying to say it wasn't like that.

Connie laughed. "I saw the way you two looked at each other at the festival dance."

Connie's remark took my breath away, because darn it, there *had* been a moment at the dance. A moment I'd been trying to forget ever since.

"Don't worry, your secret's safe with me."

I opened my mouth to protest but ended up

mumbling a thank you and a Happy Halloween as I slipped back out of the shop.

I closed my eyes and took a calming breath. The festival dance. I cringed as I remembered that fateful night...

I was riding the high from pulling the fall festival off without a hitch. Sure, the weeks leading up to it were a nightmare, and it was touch and go there for a while, but the festival itself was a success. Turnout had been spectacular, even better than I expected, with visitors pouring in both days. Sales were through the roof too, from what my friends told me. It might even have been enough to put every shop back in the black and give business owners hope for the future. Silverlake was back on the map, and for all the right reasons, despite murder and mayhem's best efforts.

Misty, Vance, Peter, and I were celebrating at Wishing Well Park on the event's final night. The band, Witches Highway, had whipped the crowd into a frenzy, with Misty and I jigging our hearts out while Peter and Vance looked on in humorous appreciation. For the record, I can't jig to save my life. Anyone watching us, and believe me, quite a few people were (including Mrs. Potts, my second-grade teacher, and the rest of the Simmering Sisters) would think we were drunk. But I promise you, the only thing we were drunk on was apple cider and kettle corn.

But then Witches Highway slowed things down.

And before I knew it, I was in Vance's arms, his

right hand was on my waist and his left hand was clasped with mine. We fit together like two pieces of a puzzle as we swayed across the dance floor.

"Go out with me." The words rushed out of Vance's mouth and sent me crashing back down to earth.

The brave, new Angelica wanted to say yes. To throw caution to the wind and give things a go with Vance one more time, because darn it, I cared for him, and sometimes, when I was alone with my thoughts and honest with myself, I wanted him back so much that it made my heart ache.

And that's what scared me.

How desperate Vance left me feeling.

I couldn't get swept away in his promises again and be left broken when he decided to break things off.

So, with my back straight and my head held high, I explained to Vance that I didn't think that was such a good idea, that we were better off remaining friends. And when the song ended, and we stepped apart, I couldn't help but think I'd made a terrible mistake.

That was nearly two months ago.

I thought about Vance all the way back to the bookstore, but all thoughts of him vanished when I stepped back inside Spellbinding Books.

It was chaos at its finest, and Misty was perfectly in control of it all. Employees were directed to their stations as guests filed in.

The decorations looked great, including the cauldron, which Misty had moved outside. With its battery-operated green LED light and overflowing dry ice blowing out into the evening air, the cauldron was the perfect touch.

"Nice cauldron."

I looked down at the cast-iron piece in tow and was about to say something when Misty said, "Can you do me a favor?"

"Sure." I had planned to disappear into the back and change into my costume, but that would only take a moment. "What do you need?"

"I forgot to grab the candied apples and pumpkin truffles from The Candy Cauldron." Misty's expression looked pained, and I was pretty sure mine mirrored hers. Luke's treats were that good. It wouldn't be a party without his chocolate confections.

"Let me change, and then I'll run out."

"You're a lifesaver. Thank you!"

TWO

Within a few minutes, I'd ditched the cauldron, donned my red cape, and dashed back out the door. Halloween decorations in the shops of Village Square were on full display. Each of the storybook stores rose to the occasion. Candles flickered from jack-o-lanterns, fake cobwebs clung to front bushes that were highlighted by purple flood-lights, and ghosts swayed in the breeze blowing in from the lake. Across the street, an enormous hay maze had taken over Wishing Well Park courtesy of the city council—even if the mayor hadn't approved of the plan. Mayor Parrish was known to disapprove all ideas that weren't her own. And she had no problem telling you so.

I was thinking of Mayor Parish when something fluttered above me, dangerously close to my head.

Were those bats? I looked up, and sure enough, they were. The animals flew off into the night, moonlight reflecting off their wings, along with something else.

Could it be sequins?

They looked like sequins based on the unnatural way the bats glittered and sparkled against the darkened sky. I decided that flying, sequined bats would be crazy and shook away the prospect while picking up my pace.

A line snaked out the door at the candy shop, The Candy Cauldron. It appeared to be the first stop for all the incoming trick-or-treaters. No one could resist the pull of the saltwater taffy that was being mechanically stretched in the front window. I knew I couldn't. The sticky orange candy was twisted and pulled until it was uniform in color and consistency. It was mesmerizing to watch. Or maybe it was the smell of the homemade fudge as it cooled on the marble countertop that people couldn't resist. Rocky Road was my favorite flavor and the shop's specialty. The sweet treat was rich and creamy, packed with peanuts and marshmallows. My mouth watered just thinking about it.

I cut in line, walking around the princesses, superheroes, ghosts, cowboys, and their parents and snuck inside. Glass display cases filled three out of the four sides of the rectangular-shaped store. The entire back wall was stacked with candy sold by the pound. Bin after bin full of brightly colored hard candies, gummies, and suckers invited patrons to grab a scooper and fill up a bag. I spotted my second favorite candy—mini gummy frogs—with their bright, neon-colored tops and marshmallow bottoms and considered buying a scoop or two but thought better of it. Aunt Thelma might not appreciate it at the moment. I hoped Clemmie had been able to help. Regardless, it would be a while before I looked at frog candy the same.

Fudge pralines made from pecans harvested right outside the door and truffles dusted with cocoa powder were just some of the homemade confections Luke, the owner of The Candy Cauldron, special-ized in. Speaking of which, Luke was dashing to and fro behind the counter, boxing up orders and ringing them up at warp speed. But no matter how fast he worked, the line never got shorter. Luke caught my eye as I stood off to the side, much like a bartender does at a packed club on a Friday night, but instead of slinging drinks, he was slinging chocolate. A much better gig, in my opinion.

"Misty sent me to grab the bookstore's order," I said over the crowd.

"Right. In the back." As Luke spoke, a loud crash came from the kitchen. He cringed. "Beatrice and Sabrina are back there, working." The way he emphasized the last word told me they were doing anything but.

"Tonight? I can't believe they're not out trick-or-treating." I knew Luke's twin nieces, Sabrina and Beatrice, from the bookstore. They came in with their mom, Sally, on Saturday mornings when I stopped in to visit Misty. Sally was a nurse at the small community hospital on the other side of the lake. Saturday mornings are my official day off. I liked to spend them walking to Village Square for a coffee and scone from the bakery, La Luna, before wandering around the bookstore. Seeing I had spent the previous decade denying I was a witch (which after being raised by my aunt in Silverlake, I should have known better), I was in serious need of a witch's refresher course. Enter the world of books, where a person could learn anything if they knew how to read. I had already read through Misty's collection of charm books, and next up, I was tackling magical defense—although some may argue I should've started with protection spells given my recent ventures.

"Sally has plans, and I promised I'd take the girls around."

"That's nice of you." And not surprising. Luke was always there for his sister.

"You say that now, but wait until I tell you what they are."

I cocked my head, waiting for Luke to continue, but he turned back to his customer instead to finish their order.

I stood patiently to the side as Luke boxed up a few pralines, waiting until he could continue our conversation.

I raised my eyebrows when he turned his attention back to me.

"She has a date with Vance," Luke clicked his tongue on the roof of his mouth as if he couldn't believe it.

I opened my mouth, unsure what I was going to say. The polite response should've been, *Good for her*, or some other nonsense. But no matter how hard I tried, I couldn't force the words form my lips.

Thankfully, Luke's attention was pulled to the next customer in line, which was a good thing. No one else needed to see my shocked expression, which I quickly replaced with a tight-lipped smile after snapping my jaw shut.

Luke stole a glance my way.

I coughed. "I think that's great," I finally managed to say, hoping my voice didn't sound as strained as it felt. I liked Sally, truly, and Vance was a nice guy, so I should be happy they're going out. But there was a solid distinction between how you should feel and how you actually felt.

"Anyway, I don't think the girls are going to make it out tonight." Luke looked around the store.

"Halloween and candy go hand-in-hand, don't they?" The line behind me continued to grow.

"They do, and add to the fact that we're short

staffed and busier than ever..." Luke's voice trailed off as he stared at the line growing longer by the second. I knew he had to get back to work. I would volunteer to lend him a hand if I wasn't already helping down at the bookstore. I was sure Aunt Thelma would too if she wasn't croaking. I supposed I could ask Percy if he was free, but despite Aunt Thelma's insistence that Percy had matured, I had yet to see it. And a poltergeist in a candy store on Halloween spelled disaster. But maybe I could help in another way.

"I can run in the back and grab the order for you, and your nieces are more than welcome to come down to the party at the bookstore. Maybe it'll keep them out of trouble?"

"If they want to, that would be great."

"Okay, I'll see." I got out of the way and let Luke get back to work.

The kitchen of The Candy Cauldron was a chocolate lover's dream come true. The countertops were full of hardening Halloween chocolates, and if the front of the shop smelled delicious, the back of the shop smelled divine. On one countertop alone, I spotted miniature white chocolate pumpkins, chocolate pretzel skeletons, and pointed witches' hats that I bet were filled with ganache or something else sinfully wonderful.

"See what it tastes like if you add caramel," Sabrina said to her sister Beatrice.

"No, let's try sea salt," Beatrice replied.

"No, caramel."

"Nooo, sea salt."

"Caramel."

"Sea salt."

"Caramel."

"Sea salt!"

"CARAMEL!" Sabrina flat-out shouted.

"Girls!" I interrupted the argument, making my presence known. The young girls snapped their attention my way. I cleared my throat. "Maybe you could try both?" I suggested hesitantly.

The girls were silent for a heartbeat until Sabrina exclaimed, "That's a great idea!"

I breathed a sigh of relief.

My relief was short lived.

"But add the sea salt first," Beatrice's voice had an edge to it. It wasn't a request.

My breath caught as I waited for them to start arguing again. But Sabrina stopped whisking the chocolate long enough for Beatrice to sprinkle some salt in.

"Now the caramel," Sabrina said, her voice just as measured. She carefully drizzled in two heaping spoonfuls of the sticky, sweet sauce.

I watched the girls, who were about ten years old and dressed up as witches with black gauzy gowns and pointed hats sitting askew on their red, curly hair, add the special ingredients to their chocolate until they were satisfied with their creation.

Beatrice began to roll the mixture into balls, placing them on the baking sheet beside her to cool.

The girls seemed perfectly content to ignore me. In fact, I wasn't even sure if they knew I was still standing there.

"Your uncle said you were busy back here," I said, interrupting them.

"Uh-huh," they said in unison, not bothering to look up.

Sabrina's brow twisted in concentration as she too molded the candy balls.

"You guys are pretty good chocolatiers."

"I know." Beatrice's voice was filled with pride. She looked up at me, beaming.

"Want to try our new caramel chocolate truffles?" Sabrina asked, holding out a small mound of chocolate.

"With sea salt," Beatrice added, sprinkling more salt on the chocolate cooling beside them.

"Um, sure. Can I take one with me?"

"Sure! Let me box that right up for you!" Sabrina hopped down from the barstool and retrieved a small white box from below the counter. It looked to be where Luke stored all of the extra packaging materials. Sabrina popped open the box like a pro. I had a feeling it would only be a matter of time before the girls worked at the shop for real.

"Thank you," I took the box from Sabrina. "Listen, the bookstore is having a Halloween party tonight. There's candy, costumes, and spooky stories. Do you guys want to come? Your uncle said it was okay."

"Nah," the girls said at the same time, not even bothering to look at one another.

"We're having too much fun here," Beatrice added.

"Are you sure? There's lots of candy," I said.

Beatrice eyed all the chocolate cooling around them. "That's okay. I think we're covered."

"Yeah, totally," Sabrina echoed the sentiment.

Beatrice retrieved a fresh metal bowl from under the kitchen counter and scooped an overflowing cup of milk chocolate disks into it. I overheard the words pumpkin and truffles.

"Well, if you change your mind, the party lasts until nine o'clock," I said.

"Okay, thanks, Angelica," Sabrina said.

"Yeah, thanks."

"You're welcome. Now can either one of you point me to the bookstore's order? It's candy apples and pumpkin truffles."

"Oh, I can."

It was Beatrice this time who hopped down and led me to a giant refrigerator. Inside, Misty's order was boxed up and ready to go. I could see the apples and truffles through the clear plastic lid of the top box before it fogged up from the change in temperature. When Misty said candy apples, she really meant apples covered in candy. I was expecting to see traditional red glazed apples, but these were above and beyond that. These ginormous apples were loaded with caramel and topped with candy bar pieces and drizzled with white and dark chocolate. I was definitely going to have to try one tonight.

When we stepped out of the fridge, Sabrina had replaced the milk chocolate disks with white chocolate ones.

"White chocolate?" Beatrice scrunched up her face in disgust.

"I'm tired of milk chocolate," Sabrina said. The white disks were already starting to melt over the double boiler.

"But white chocolate is gross," Beatrice said flatly.

"It is not."

"Is too."

"Is not."

"Is too!"

"Girls?" I attempted to interrupt the building argument, but they kept right on going, talking right over me.

"Why do you always do that?" Beatrice asked.

"Do what?" Sabrina fisted her hands on her hips.

"Try and tell me what to do!"

"I'm not telling you what to do. I'm telling you

what I'm going to do. And I'm using white chocolate."

"Girls." My voiced was louder and sterner this time.

It didn't matter.

"You think you're the boss of me, but you're not." Beatrice's voice turned shrill.

"But *I am* the boss." Sabrina had the nerve to roll her eyes at her sister.

In hindsight, that was the wrong thing to do.

"Oooh!" Beatrice scrunched up her fists. In the next instant, she scooped up a handful of not quite hardened chocolates and chucked them at her sister. They smacked Sabrina right on the cheek. The chocolate smeared her face and plopped to the ground.

"Beatrice!" I shouted in shock.

Sabrina wasted no time. I thought she'd retaliate by throwing chocolate back. But she snatched out her wand faster than I could say Happy Halloween. In an instant, she shot her sister in the face with an engorgement charm. Beatrice's nose grew by the second, making the child look ghastly.

Beatrice's hands shot up to her face, trying to keep her nose in place.

"Sabrina!" she shouted, sounding extremely nasally.

I set the candied apples down and fumbled for my wand, to reverse the spell.

Luke popped his head in at that second. "Did you find them?" he asked before taking in the chaos.

I looked back at him wide-eyed. "I...ah..."

"Sabrina!" Luke said as he saw Beatrice's face. He gave Sabrina a disappointed look before whipping out his wand, pointing it at Beatrice and saying, "Tixie."

The young witch's nose popped back to normal.

"She started it," Sabrina grumbled in defense.

"I did not!"

"Did too!"

"Did not!"

"Enough. Do I need to call your mom?" Luke asked.

Both girls snapped their mouths shut and crossed their arms over their chests.

"Sorry about that," Luke said to me. I was going to say that it was alright, when Luke spotted the bookstore's order. "You found it."

"Yes, thank you. I better get going."

"And I better have a word with my nieces." Luke eyed them sternly.

"You guys are still more than welcome to come down to the bookstore," I added as I picked the bookstore's order back up. Although I wasn't sure if they'd be any better behaved down there.

"We'll see about that," Luke said, crossing his arms to match the girls'.

I slipped out of the kitchen and heard the girls

arguing, I mean, stating their sides of the story, before I even made it five steps. I closed my eyes briefly, feeling sorry for Luke if that was how it was going to go for him the rest of the night. Yikes. Whatever his sister was paying him to babysit, it wasn't enough. Not even close.

THREE

With my hands full, I left the candy shop and started back towards the bookstore. All around me, kids called out trick-or-treat as they skipped from shop to shop collecting their goodies. I smiled at families as I weaved down the path and side-stepped the eager children.

"Molly! Can you hear me?" Council member and town guardian, Michael McCormick's voice echoed across the parking lot and stole my attention. "Molly? Anyone?" The councilman continued to yell at the entrance of the hay maze. I was standing in front of the bookstore. A vampire was walking towards me, well, a witch in a vampire costume. At least I hoped he was a witch dressed as a vampire. Real vampires scared me. Heck, they even scared Vance. Not that I knew any in real life. They tended to keep to themselves.

The man looked vaguely familiar, but it was hard to place him with the slicked back hair, pointy fangs, and billowing satin cape.

"Are you going to the party?" I asked the fake vampire, motioning to the bookstore.

"Yes-th," the vampire replied, his large fangs making it hard for him to articulate properly, which only confirmed my suspicion. I'd never heard of a vampire's fangs causing a lisp. That, and no real vamp would wear a cape that cheesy. It was red satin on the inside, black on the outside, with a thick collar turned upright and tied shut at the neck with a bow.

"Can you give these to Misty? She's probably behind the register." I held the boxes out to him, not giving the vampire much of a choice.

"Sh-ure thing." The vampire took the boxes from my arms.

"Thanks, I appreciate it. Tell her Angelica will be back in a minute." I tugged my cloak tighter around me and jogged across the parking lot to the maze.

The sun had set entirely by this point, making the once innocent maze now appear foreboding. The hay had been stacked at least four bales high, creating walls eight feet tall. Somewhere in the middle was the town's three-tiered fountain, complete with a witch statue, but even that was blocked from sight. The surrounding pecan trees cast eerie shadows in the moonlight. A mist settled in the air, adding to the spooky atmosphere. Mr.

McCormick paced before the entrance, repeatedly calling for his daughter, Molly, or anyone else who could hear him.

"Is everything okay?" I asked.

Mr. McCormick came to an abrupt stop. "No, it's not okay," the usually calm councilman was flushed with worry. "No one's come out of the maze. They're all lost in there."

"Aren't they supposed to be for a little bit? It's a maze after all," I tried to rationalize.

"You don't understand. Fifteen people have walked in that maze, and not one of them has come out." Mr. McCormick pointed to the exit that was right next to him. "Molly went in to figure out what was going on twenty minutes ago, and now she's lost too."

"Did you try giving her cell phone a call?" I reached in my pocket for mine.

"Oh, I don't carry one of those things."

Thankfully I did, but I didn't know Molly's number, and Mr. McCormick didn't know it off the top of his head either. The man was old school, preferring magic to technology. With my phone still out, I turned on the flashlight app and walked a couple steps into the maze.

A chill crept up my spine, growing colder with each step, which I had to admit, were getting harder and harder to take.

My instincts told me to turn tail and get out of

there. Mr. McCormick was right, something was wrong.

Or maybe I was just a big baby, and the spooky atmosphere was getting the best of me.

After the first turn, everything in front of me was pitch black and dead silent. The phone's beam wasn't strong enough to pierce the overwhelming darkness. I wasn't sure you could get me to walk further in that maze even if you paid me, that's how creeped out I was at that moment.

"I told you this was a bad idea." Mayor Parrish's voice said from behind me.

"What, celebrating Halloween?" I retorted as I walked backwards to the entrance, not turning my back to the darkness for a second.

"Well, no, but like this," Mayor Parrish motioned to the Halloween hijinks going on around us. If you were quiet, you could hear more than one person croaking over at the Village Square, and this time, when the bats flew overhead, I took a solid look and realized they were in fact made out of sequins.

"Okay, so minus a few croaking citizens and a couple wayward decorations, I think tonight has been a smashing success." I was lying through my teeth, but I didn't want to give Mayor Parish the satisfaction of knowing she was right. Maybe I was stubborn, or just a bit too proud, but it would take a lot more mayhem before I'd conceded her point. Mayor Parrish's idea of a Halloween party was night and day from mine. Forget trick-or-treating, the mayor would much prefer to sit around an electric gas fireplace with a cashmere throw draped around her shoulders, nibbling pumpkin truffles with zero kids around. That's the vision she had for Silverlake, and she expected everyone to fall in line, which people were starting to do until I moved back into town.

"I'd expect this type of foolishness in Harrisville. Not Silverlake," the mayor continued, referencing the nearby non-magical city which was known for its small-town charm and spectacular Halloween festival. That was because their mayor was in fact a witch who knew how to make the holidays truly magical, and he took advantage of that fact.

"One would think we could learn a thing or two from our mortal neighbors," I replied coolly.

Mayor Parrish actually snorted her response before walking off. I turned away from her backside and looked down the darkened corridor once more, hoping someone would make an appearance, but they didn't.

Okay, change in plans. "I need to pop in the bookstore for a minute, and then I'll come back and figure out what's going on here. Hopefully, the maze is just a bit trickier than people expected, and everyone will start filing out soon. But, in the meantime, don't let anyone else enter."

"Good idea," Mr. McCormick said. I would have

given the councilman my cell phone number and asked him to call me with news if he had a phone.

"I'll be back as soon as I can." I turned on my heel and was halfway back to the bookstore when my text message tone went off. Make that four text messages in rapid succession. Hoping it was Aunt Thelma with good news about her curse, I took my phone out of my pocket and saw that the messages were in fact from Aunt Thelma, and it wasn't good news.

Help!

Come to the tea shop.

Quick!

Emergency!!!

I shot back a text that I was on my way. There was no sense in calling. If Aunt Thelma was still croaking, she wouldn't be able to tell me what was going on. I needed to get to her as quickly as possible.

A mix of dread and panic washed over me as I pocketed my phone and took off in a sprint across the parking lot and through the village shops to Sit For a Spell. I leapt over garden mums, dashed around pumpkins, and threw apologies over my shoulder to the trick-or-treaters in my mad dash to reach my aunt.

The quaint tea shop was known for its magical herbal remedies as much as it was for its giftshop and delectable afternoon tea service. It was the perfect shop to go to if you needed to put together a get-well gift or host a bridal shower, both of which were common at Sit For a Spell. Emergencies were few and far between.

"Everything okay?" Diane, the owner of La Luna Bakery yelled to me as I raced past the bakery. She was half outside, her yellow apron glowing from the overhead light, holding the door open for customers.

"I don't know!" I hollered back honestly, not slowing down.

"Call me!" Diane yelled.

I nodded that I would and hoped Diane had seen the motion in the darkness with me moving so fast. I knew what Diane meant too. The bakery might be busy, but all I needed to do was call her if I needed help, and she'd drop everything and meet me at Clemmie's. That's just the type of witch she was, always willing to help a friend. That night, when I was counting my blessings, I'd have to remember how thankful I was that she was in my life.

As I came closer to Clemmie's, my mind raced with the possibilities of what could be wrong, but nothing prepared me for what I saw when I arrived at the shop's doorstep.

The best way to describe it was utter chaos.

I was so shocked, I couldn't move. I just stood there and stared through the front window, taking it all in.

Bright purple pixies, about the size of my hand, flew about the tea shop, throwing loose-leaf tea around like confetti. Electric blue flashes shot out from Clemmie's wand as she attempted to freeze the pixies with poor success. Icicles hung down from the ceiling, and frost clouded the bottom of the front window.

Aunt Thelma was apparently still croaking because she had ditched the spells and was running around trying to catch the pixies with her bare hands. An impossible feat, but that didn't stop her from trying. The fairies with their big round eyes, pointed ears, and oversized wings, were devilishly fast. From outside the window, I heard their child-like laughter as they destroyed Clemmie's tea shop with aplomb. The outside shop sign had been switched to closed, but the door was ajar courtesy of a broken teapot, keeping the door from shutting properly.

I took a deep breath and charged in, racing toward the checkout counter, shielding my head the entire time. My feet slipped on the wet floor from the melting icicles, making it hard to run at full speed.

The flutter of the pixie's wings sounded like a swarm of bees. They zipped everywhere at once. The only thing louder than the whirring of their wings was their laughter. They sounded like a group of toddlers caught in a giggle fit.

The pixies were clearly having *fun*.

I ducked behind the counter in the nick of time, crouching low, my knees tucked to my chest. Two of the pixies had teamed up and thrown a ceramic mug my way. The cup hit the wall behind me and broke into chunky pieces.

"Hey now!" Clemmie roared, hands on her hips. "You stop that this instant!"

A second mug flew past her. Clemmie gasped as it barely missed her and crashed into the self-service tea station, hitting the sugar bowl and scattering crystals across the countertop.

Clemmie moved faster than she had in years, hightailing it behind the counter to join me.

Aunt Thelma took cover behind a scented candle display. Sooner or later the pixies would get lucky and the mugs would hit their mark and none of us wanted it to be our head.

"Where did they come from?" I peeked above the countertop. The pixies had discovered how to operate the ceiling fan, which included the overhead lights that were now flicking off and on like a strobe light.

I glanced up. A calmer pixie, if there was such a thing, had decided to sit for a cup of tea on one of the fan blades, legs crossed and pinkie extended like a proper English miss, but the moment the fan started whirling, the pixie ditched the cup over her shoulder. The porcelain cup smashed onto the floor and she started riding the fan like a bull, complete with an imaginary lasso circling above her head.

It was like a car crash that was impossible to look away from.

Clemmie followed my line of sight. "Well, that isn't something you see every day. Little bugger."

"Where'd they come from?" I repeated my question.

"I don't know. Someone let them in the back," Clemmie replied.

The ceiling fan was whirling now on max speed. Rodeo pixie held on for dear life. A second pixie flew off from the fan and hit the front window with a thud. A chorus of laughter erupted as a line began to form, the pixies pushing one another, vying for who could ride it next.

"That's horrible," I said, referring to the mysterious pixie releaser.

"If I find out who is responsible, heaven help me," Clemmie reached for the broom on the ground, I bet for defense as much as offense, while staying low to the floor.

"RIBBIT!" Aunt Thelma agreed.

The icicles were rapidly melting, leaving little pools of water on Clemmie's wood floors. A separate group of pixies splashed in the puddles, jumping and stomping as they sent droplets of water into the air.

Part of me was tempted to transform into a cat and chase the pixies out of the shop, but then they'd still be flying around Village Square. What if they found their way to the bookstore? Or the bakery? Or any of the other shops? I shuddered to imagine the chocolate fight these guys could cause at The Candy

Cauldron. If Luke thought Beatrice and Sabrina were naughty, wait until he met this rowdy bunch.

"We have to catch them," I said, coming to the only responsible conclusion.

"That's what we're trying to do!" Clemmie replied at the same time another mug crashed to the floor. "But they're too fast. I can't stun them or freeze 'em."

Clemmie was right, those two spells would've also been my go-to. They made the most sense.

"I haven't hit a single one. And your poor aunt's running herself ragged." Clemmie's voice was full of frustration.

Aunt Thelma's face was twisted into a scowl.

Too fast, huh? I looked at the pixies zipping around the shop. There had to be a spell for that. Something to slow them down, but what?

I bit my bottom lip as I thought back to the recent charm books I'd read. I knew of charms to summon lost objects, make items levitate, and I could even transform paperclips into butterflies. Although I wasn't sure how transformation spells would work on pixies, or if I was even crazy enough to try it. What if they turned into a hive of angry hornets? Or a hybrid pixie hornet? I bit my lip hard. It was too risky. With magic, you could always make things worse.

I needed a broad spell. Something that casted a wide net so to speak.

And then I thought of it. "You two stand behind me." I stood up, filled with determination. I was on a mission and acting braver than I felt. Aunt Thelma dashed over to the counter and took refuge behind me next to Clemmie. Both ladies took up their positions without comment.

I brandished my wand with all the confidence I could muster, took a deep breath, and reminded myself to believe in the magic as I shouted, "Argos!" The strong timbre of my voice sounded unnatural to my ears. The voice was commanding and unwavering. I was in charge.

A gold ray burst forth from my wand, flooding the shop with warm light, impacting all that stood before me.

Instantly, it was as if someone had drenched the pixies in molasses. Their rapid movements flicked to a standstill. A snail could move faster. Even the pixies blinking was delayed, their long lashes sweeping slowly up and down their unnaturally large eyes. The pixies struggled against their magical confinement, but no matter how much effort they put forth, their wings could only labor lazily up and down.

"A slow-motion spell, smart thinking," Clemmie said

"PLUNK," Aunt Thelma agreed. At least I think she agreed.

"Thanks." The spell was recommended for dogs that had gotten off their leash or objects that had fallen so you could catch them before they broke, but it turned out to work great on pixies. "Do you have a box?" I asked Clemmie.

"Yes, ma'am." Clemmie stood up and power walked to her storage room. She came back a moment later with a large square box that was the perfect size. I used a pair of scissors from under the counter to poke air holes in the box and together, we worked to round the pixies up.

"Not so fast now, are you?" Clemmie said while standing on a chair and fetching the remaining pixies off the ceiling fan. The pixies looked on in disbelief as she caught them with ease.

"What a mess," I eyed Clemmie's shop once the last pixie was secured. A mixture of tea leaves, water, and broken ceramics littered the floor. Clemmie's shop was always warm and inviting, which was why locals and tourists alike loved it. But right now, it was a disaster.

"Why don't you guys start picking up. I'll go to the pet shop and see if they know where these guys came from." Since the shop specialized in magical creatures, they might very well know. Worst case scenario, I could buy a more suitable enclosure to contain the pixies until we could release them back into the forest.

"I'll make some calls too. See who can lend us a hand." I knew Diane would come down. Assuming the flower shop was closing soon, I was sure Roger, Diane's boyfriend, would help too.

"Don't worry about this place. I'll see to it. You just get those little devils out of here." Clemmie thrust the box out to me.

"You got it. I'll let you know what I find out." I took one last parting look at the destruction left behind and slipped out of the shop. Clemmie walked after me, scooting the broken teapot out of the way with her foot and locking the door.

FOUR

I t's not that I had forgotten about Mr. McCormick over at the hay maze, or Misty's party at the bookstore, it's just that I was running from one fire to another. With a box full of pixies, I hightailed it to the pet store to see if they had any idea where Clemmie's mischievous visitors had come from. The Village Square was busier than I had ever seen it before. Sidewalks were clogged with children running amok, collecting as much candy as possible in the couple hours trick-or-treating lasted. I tried to ignore the chorus of frog sounds that punctuated the nighttime air which I suspected was not being produced by native amphibians, and believe me, we had plenty of those around Silverlake.

Inside, the pet shop was relatively calm compared to the chaos going on outside.

"Hey guys," I said to the two teenage boys who

were working the front counter. They both had their cell phones out, hoodies pulled up, and were engrossed in a game on their cell phones, oblivious to the real world. "You didn't, by chance, sell a bunch of pixies tonight, did you?"

"Pixies? What kind?" The first teenager glanced up. His name tag read Zach. "Oh man, did you see that dragon?" he asked his co-worker, Isaac, before I could reply.

"Was it a bat dragon?" Isaac looked over at his coworker's phone.

"Yeah, man. Wonder what it'll take for him to trade it."

"Offer him your neon kangaroo."

"No way, bro. That's a legendary."

"You can buy one on eBay."

"You got twenty bucks for one?"

"Point taken, bro."

The two continued on with their gaming talk, forgetting, or more like not caring, that I was there.

Out front, a skeleton walked past the window, and it wasn't a person in a costume. I stared at the four-foot tall, animated corpse walking by. Its body was completely see through, leaving only the bony framework. "Tell me that's a decoration," I said aloud to myself. I was pretty sure that it was, just like the sequin bats. But how it came to be walking down the street was beyond me. Silverlake had its fair share of resident ghosts, but

I'd never heard of a skeleton skipping through town.

I wondered if this is what it felt like living in the Twilight Zone.

I waited until the skeleton walked out of sight and turned my focus back to the teenage workers.

"What kind?" I repeated Zach's question, bringing the conversation back on topic and trying to get the workers' attention. "They're the purple kind." I had no idea what their official name was. I knew there were different species, but I wasn't any good at identifying them.

"North Atlantic pixies? Cool. Is that what's in the box?" Isaac asked, putting his phone down.

"It is, but I wouldn't..." Isaac reached for the box and opened it before I could complete my warning. My slow-motion spell had worn off, and the pixies zoomed out of the box and took off around the store. The pixies were angrier than a hive of hornets. They were out for revenge. They immediately tore into a bag of birdseed and began to simultaneously throw handfuls in the air and in their mouths, the seeds raining down around us. A second group of pixies flew toward the bird cages and began to work on the locks, flinging the cages open in record time.

I closed my eyes and took a calming breath. At this point, I shouldn't have been surprised by anything. I was about to take out my wand and repeat the slow-motion spell when the pet store workers handled things in their own way. Zach nonchalantly walked over to the birdcages and shut them before any birds escaped. Then he opened an empty birdcage that appeared to have been intended for a large parrot. The cage was as tall as he was and twice as wide. Isaac disappeared to the back room for a minute and returned with a bowl full of fresh fruit. The minute the dish was in the center of the cage, both boys whistled for the pixies. The creatures ditched their shenanigans and zipped right over and into the cage, their little purple faces happily devouring bits of mango and ripe, red cherries. Zach and Isaac made it look so easy. I was convinced this wasn't the first time they had caught a batch of pixies.

"That's impressive," I said, unable to keep the awe out of my voice. You could bet I'd never forget the fruit trick when it came to dealing with pixies. Not that Clemmie had any fresh fruit lying around her tea shop. At least, I didn't think she did. Fruit tea maybe.

Suddenly, something small and wet hit me on the side of my face and rolled to the floor. It was a cherry pit. I looked over to the cage where a pixie was pointing and laughing at me. "Charming." I glared at the troublesome sprite. The sarcasm was heavy in my voice.

"They're pretty awesome, aren't they?" Zach looked at the pixies lovingly, misinterpreting my comment.

"Where did you say you found them?" Isaac asked me.

"Sit For A Spell. Somebody let them loose in the tea shop. They did a fine job of destroying everything they could get their hands on."

"Yeah, they'll do that. That's why we don't carry them. They're not domesticated like a lot of the other pixies. These guys don't want to be your friend," Zach said.

"So, they didn't come from here," I surmised. Both boys shook their heads. "Any idea where they could've come from?"

Isaac spoke up. "Nothing local. They're probably imported."

"Unless they came over from Harrisville. There's a breeder that way. Strange guy," Zach added. "He comes in every now and then."

A pixie breeder? Now I'd heard everything. Scoping out an odd duck on Halloween was not my idea of a good time. I really hoped it wouldn't come to that. "Okay, thanks guys. Do you mind if I leave the pixies here?"

"Yeah, bro. That's cool," Zach replied, already reaching for his cell phone once more.

"Thanks, I appreciate it." One problem down. How many did I have left to tackle? I was too scared to count.

I said goodbye to Zach and Isaac, who were back

to talking about bat dragons before I had even walked out the door.

I started power walking back to the bookstore when I spotted Percy sneaking around one of the Village Square gardens.

There was really no other word for it. His head was bent low, hunched over as he examined a rose bush, periodically looking back up at the moon as if trying to gauge something. What, I had no idea.

My curiosity got the best of me. I stepped off the flagstone path, crossed the grassy yard, and joined Percy in the mulch.

I bent low, copying his stance, my face level with his. "Whatcha doin'?"

"Hubaba-juba!" Percy yelled with a start as he ricocheted into a standing position. His shoulders ramrod straight. "Gosh darn it, Jelly! You scared me to death."

I raised my eyebrows as I stood. "Did I now?" I folded my arms across my chest. "Can't imagine what that feels like. Honestly, I have no clue what it's like to be scared out of my whits day in and day out."

Percy scowled. "Fine, point taken. Now run along, I have things to do."

"Like what? What *have* you been up to?"

"It's really none of your business." Percy looked away from me. He couldn't have been more dismissive if he'd tried.

"True, but maybe I can help you."

Percy was silent, his thoughts playing across his face. First, he looked annoyed, then worried, and finally downright distraught. I suddenly realized that Percy did need my help, whether he was willing to admit it or not.

I stopped worrying about curses, rogue mazes, and wayward decorations for a moment, and gave the poltergeist my full attention. "Percy, what's wrong?" I kept my voice gentle and judgement-free.

Percy seemed unsure. I thought he was going to shut down and disappear, or tell me to mind my own business again. But he surprised me. "Do you...do you think this rose was planted under a full moon?" Gone was the trickster ghost, and all that remained was the older gentleman Percy was when he had passed.

"What?" Whatever I had expected Percy to ask, that wasn't it.

Percy was waiting for my response. It was as if my answer would unlock a mystery that he was desperate to solve.

"Um, I'm not sure." I looked around the garden as if it held the answer while trying to remember if anyone in town might know. "I suppose we could ask Mr. McCormick." As a town elder and horticulturist, he might possibly have the answer. He was really the only person I could think of. I followed Percy's eyes as he looked back up at the moon. "It's full right now."

Percy looked over at me, hope filling his eyes.

"I know a lot of spells require ingredients harvested under a full moon," I continued, not sure what Percy was up to, but suspecting magic was somehow involved. A ghost didn't ask about curses and flowers harvested under a full moon without it being magic-related. I'd read about full-moon harvests more than once in my recent studies. For example, re-animation spells usually required mandrake root that had been harvested under a full moon to be maximally effective. The author had gone on to claim that if found growing under a gallows, it would be even better. I scrunched my face at the memory of *that* author's note. I'd yet to come across a spell that specified the moon phase for planting, but I supposed it was possible. Again, Mr. McCormick would be the man to ask.

I said as much to Percy. "Mr. McCormick is working the hay maze. I'm headed back over there. Want me to ask him about the rose?"

Percy gave a curt nod. "I, ah, have a couple other items I'm rounding up. If you don't mind, could I meet up with you in a little bit?"

"Sure, that works," I said after a moment. It took my mind a second to catch up to this new version of Percy. "I'll most likely be at the hay maze or the bookstore."

Percy looked back down at the rose, then to me, and then winked out of existence. I felt the quick tug on my hair a second later, Percy's signature move. It was nice to see that the poltergeist hadn't completely changed.

I stood still for a second and then shook my head, wondering what other surprises the night might have in store for me.

I shouldn't have asked. No sooner had the thought passed my consciousness did my cell phone ring.

At this point I was scared to even look at it.

Reluctantly, I took out my phone and looked to see who the caller was. I found myself staring at the display.

Vance was calling me.

The first questions that came to mind were: Why was Vance calling me? Wasn't he supposed to be on a date?

The second, or I suppose the third question was: Was I going to answer it?

Who was I kidding? Of course I was going to.

Because no matter how awkward I'd left things with him, Vance was still my friend. And just like with Diane being willing to drop everything and help me tonight, I'd do the same for Vance.

I hit the green answer button. "Hello?"

From the other end, I was greeted by a loud, hollow thumping sound. Like something heavy repeatedly hitting a window.

"Not the window," Vance said to someone unknown.

"Vance, you there? Is everything okay?" I stopped walking and plugged my opposite ear with my fingertip so I could hear better.

Now it sounded like something heavy scrapping across the hardwood floor.

"Vance, can you hear me?"

"Angie?" Vance seemed to finally realize that our lines had connected.

"Yeah, what's going on?"

"Hang on." More loud scrapping sounds filled the background for a solid minute. I stood patiently off to the side, smiling at trick-or-treaters as they paraded by. "Hopefully that'll keep him," Vance muttered.

"Keep who?" But Vance wasn't listening to me. "Vance?"

"Sorry."

"What is going on?"

"You're not going to believe this, but there's a gargoyle outside my door."

"What?" I cocked my head, thinking I misheard what Vance said. "What's outside your door?"

"A gargoyle," Vance shouted over the thumping sound in the background.

"A gargoyle?" A deep growl rumbled in the background. It sent shivers up my spine. "How is that even possible?"

"I have no idea, but he's big, and he's angry, and I have to figure out what to do before he breaks down my door."

"Did you call the sheriff?" Sheriff Reynolds was arrogant and cocky and the last person I usually wanted to talk to, well him and his daughter, but given the circumstances, a phone call to the sheriff's department was warranted. Maybe Vance would get lucky, and Deputy Jones would answer. He was an officer on our side.

"I was trying not to. He's been passing out citations left and right. My phone hasn't quit ringing all night." Vance was a defense attorney, and Sheriff Reynolds loved ticketing people. "I thought it was a statue I could disable with a spell, but that's not working. Magic ricochets off it."

I tried to think if I knew any spells that would help, but I hadn't read anything about stopping animated statues in any books. "You're sure it's a statue?"

"Pretty sure. I think it belongs to the church across the street."

I thought of the church's architecture and remembered they had a gargoyle or two perched up top. "Like the decorations," I mumbled under my breath.

"What's that?"

I was getting ready to tell Vance about the bat

and skeleton, but the thumping on the other end of the line suddenly got louder.

"I have to go. He's on the roof," Vance said.

"Call the sheriff!" I said before our lines disconnected. I had no idea if he had heard me or how I was going to help him, but I knew I had to try.

FIVE

I called Misty on my way around the lake. She didn't answer, and that didn't surprise me since I knew how busy the store was. I decided to text her once I was parked to fill her in on what was going on outside her front door.

As I rounded the lake and came up to the residential district, I gulped at the sight of a gargoyle sitting perched on top of the town's single stoplight. It sat on the metal bar like an oversized pigeon, and I do mean oversized. I never realized how large the cathedral's gargoyles were, nor had I bothered to count them. How many were currently flying around Silverlake?

Unfortunately, the only way to Vance's office was to drive under the gargoyle and turn right. I crouched low in the car, and hit the gas as I made the turn, crossing my fingers the concrete beast wouldn't jump down and land on my roof and crush me in the process.

The gargoyle was, thankfully, content to remain at his post. It may have growled at me as I passed underneath, but perhaps it had been my imagination. If I could have looked past the madness for a moment, I would've been able to appreciate how much Silverlake had risen to the challenge of making this the most festive Halloween ever. Purple and green twinkling lights outlined the post office's front window. A spirited scene of jack-o'-lanterns and falling leaves had been painted on the bank's glass doors. Pumpkins were on every porch. The sense of community was oddly comforting and something I hadn't realized I'd missed living in Chicago. It wasn't that long ago that I'd called the Windy City home and that Silverlake had been a sleepy town facing bankruptcy. Tourism here had dried up, and businesses had almost been forced to close if something wasn't done about it. On a whim, I suggested hosting a fall festival, and the rest was history.

A scarecrow walked in front of my car and snapped me back to the present. I slammed on my brakes. The decoration had a metal pie plate for a face, straw for hair, and was sporting a pair of overalls on its stick frame. It turned its head a hundred and eighty degrees and looked straight at me with its black permanent marker-drawn eyes. I ducked down in my seat. I should have floored it and ran the thing over, but I was too freaked out.

After crossing the street, the decoration continued down the sidewalk. "Okay, now that is creepy." I slowly sat back up and shivered, instantly annoyed. Someone was clearly out to sabotage Halloween and make it so Silverlake never wanted to celebrate the witchiest holiday of the year again, because let's face it, no one wants a scarecrow knocking on their front door. It rated right up there with dolls coming to life. I shivered again.

No, this went above and beyond a Halloween prank. Croaking was one thing, but decorations and statues coming to life and pixies trashing stores were another. Not to mention the hay maze. I crossed my fingers Mr. McCormick had jumped the gun there, but I couldn't deny that the maze had me on edge. The thought of running into that scarecrow in there? Well, that was the stuff of horror movies. Not cool, anonymous trickster, not cool. Clemmie was right, the person responsible for all this better watch out when I discover who they are--and believe me, I will discover them.

Up ahead, the town's firetruck was parked on the side of the street. The firefighters were hanging out the open cab, wands out on alert, scanning the horizon. I was afraid to ask, but forewarned is forearmed, or so they say. I rolled down my window as I passed by. "What's wrong?" I asked Fire Chief Grady, not bothering to say hello.

"Spiders," the chief said. He kept his eyes on the road.

"Come again?"

"We have a report of giant spiders in the area."

"Oh, no. How big?"

"Big." The fire chief held his hands out in a circle about the size of a basketball.

I visibly paled, and my palms turned sweaty. I take that back. I'd rather face a scarecrow in the maze than a pack of man-eating spiders. This was officially the Halloween of horrors.

"Is it a spelled decoration?" I asked, hopefully.

"I don't know." The chief looked like he hadn't thought of that.

"That's what's going on over at Village Square. Plus, I just saw a scarecrow walking down the street."

The chief relayed the message to his crew while I idled beside them. "Try tixi first. If not, hypnos might work." Hypnos was the spell for putting something to sleep. I hadn't thought of that one. "Worst case, freeze the suckers until we figure out what to do with them."

Chief Grady turned back to me, and I wished him luck before adding, "I'm going to see a man about a gargoyle."

It was the fire chief's turn to look apprehensive. "A real gargoyle?"

"Trying to break into Vance's office, and there's one perched on top of the stoplight down there."

Chief Grady sighed. I knew exactly how he felt. "I'll call it in. Stay safe."

"Will do." I motored up my window and moved forward, eyes peeled for any giant spiders, sequined bats, or creepy scarecrows. With my eyes still on the road, I dug my wand out of my pocket. Wand in hand, I gripped the steering wheel and proceeded with caution, which was something I should have done from the get-go.

A few minutes later I'd reached my destination.

"What was I thinking?" I asked myself as I pulled into the public parking lot that served the surrounding businesses. I parked in the spot next to Vance's pickup truck and looked over and up to the cathedral where the gargoyles had come from. Over at Vance's office, something formidable rustled in the bushes. Even from inside my car, I heard the unmistakable sound of an animal growling. In the darkness, a set of red glowing eyes locked with mine, and I gasped.

"Think about Vance." I reminded myself of my friend who was trapped in his office.

At least, I thought he was.

I called Vance next.

"Hey," he answered, sounding a little out of breath.

"You still prisoner in your office?"

"Unfortunately. The gargoyle keeps looking in the window for me and growling."

"Sheriff on his way?"

"No, I can't get through. Line's always busy." I shouldn't be surprised that the sheriff's department line was busy. We were a little town without a central dispatch. If you wanted the sheriff, you called his office. With all the Halloween hijinks, I was sure the phone was ringing off the hook.

"I moved my desk against the window and barricaded the door with my filing cabinet," Vance added.

"Okay. I'm here out front."

"Do you see it?"

I looked back at the red glowing eyes and visibly swallowed. "Uh-huh. Give me a minute to think, and I'll call you back, okay?"

"I'll be here."

I hung up with Vance and sat alone with my thoughts for a moment. The coward in me wanted to put the car in reverse and burn rubber, but I couldn't do that to Vance. He needed my help and who knew how long the authorities would take to arrive. Vance couldn't even get through to them. I tried to think about what I knew about gargoyles. Let's see, they were a staple of Gothic architecture, and they served as waterspouts. "Not helpful," I chastised myself. Unfortunately, I hadn't read up on magical creatures. If I had, I might've known about the pixie's apparent love for fruit.

"Come on, think. There has to be something." Vance said his spells were ricocheting off the gargoyles stone exterior, but there had to be something that could stop them. I thought back to mythology and how gargoyles were placed around churches to remind people of the evil outside. Gargoyles were also said to fly at night, returning to their posts and into stone when the sun rose.

"That's it! Sunlight turns gargoyles back into stone." But that realization was met with a frown. Daylight was at least ten hours away. I didn't want Vance remaining prisoner until morning. I didn't think he'd want to be stuck in his office all night either. Not with his date tonight.

"Wait, I know how to solve this."

I sprang from my car before I could talk myself out of my plan. Wand drawn, I marched forward. As soon as I got close enough, I was going to blast the area with a sunlight spell and pray that it did the job.

The sunlight wouldn't lighten the atmosphere for long, but I was hoping to at least stun the gargoyle.

Perhaps my plan had been a bit overzealous.

The gargoyle emerged from the bushes before I was even in striking distance. He was stocky like a bulldog, with jowls to match. He had wings like a bat and a tail like a devil.

In an instant, the gargoyle charged. His four legs thundered down the sidewalk. I knew what spell I was supposed to say, but at that moment, I panicked.

Everyone always talks about instincts and fight or flight, but no one ever mentions freeze, but that's what happened. I froze. I might as well have had ice blocks for feet because I wasn't going anywhere. It was as if I had been spelled into place.

The gargoyle ran straight for me.

I braced for impact.

Jumping up, the gargoyle's massive front paws hit my thighs and knocked me backward. It was like trying to catch a cinder block. I hit the ground hard. My palms caught my fall, but before I could sit up to defend myself, the gargoyle's paws were on my chest, pushing down. The air went out of my lungs in a whoosh. The weight of him kept me down, and I couldn't move. It had happened in the blink of an eye.

I stared up into the beast's glowing red eyes and thought: This is it. Death by gargoyle. On Halloween no less. It was the stuff of urban legend.

Drool dripped from the gargoyle's mouth, and I turned away, not willing to stare down my fate.

Two things happened in the next instant, both of which I will never forget. One, Vance came running out of his office, carrying his office chair above his head and screaming like a banshee. And two, the gargoyle dropped a fist-sized rock on my chest before sitting back patiently, wagging his tail.

I lay there stunned.

The gargoyle let out a playful bark.

Vance stopped mid-stride.

Slowly I sat up. The rock tumbled from my chest. I picked it up and scrambled to sit up. The gargoyle's ears perked up, and his tail wagged in earnest.

"Is this what you want?" I hesitantly held up the rock in my hand. The gargoyle pranced in anticipation like a super-charged pit bull. "You want me to throw it?" Again with the tail wagging and drool, only this time, it went everywhere when he shook his head in excitement.

I chucked the rock, and the gargoyle tore off after it.

"Hurry, before he comes back," Vance said, reaching for my hand. But before we could take two steps, the gargoyle was back. He dropped the rock at my feet and sat expectantly like a good boy.

I picked up the rock and threw it again. The gargoyle retrieved it in lightning speed a second time. That wasn't an exaggeration, the gargoyle was supernaturally fast.

After the third time, the gargoyle dropped the rock and proceeded to roll on his back in the grass, his devilish tail swishing back and forth.

"This is what had you trapped in your office this whole time?" I bent down and scratched the gargoyle between his ears. He playfully licked my hand, his bat wings spread out behind him.

"Like you didn't think he was going to rip your throat out." Vance tried to be serious, but even he couldn't hide the amusement in his voice at the turn of events.

"Well, we know better now. The question is, what do we do next?"

"I think we should name him Rocky," Vance said.

"What? You can't keep the gargoyle." I looked over at Vance like he couldn't be serious.

"What, why not?" Vance looked down lovingly at his new pet.

"Because..." I struggled to come up with a reason. I finally settled on, "Because he belongs to the church."

"Well, he's not going to go stand guard right now. We might as well bring him with us and keep him out of trouble." Vance looked rather proud of his rationale.

I hated to admit it, but that actually made sense.

"Fine, but we're taking your truck." Rocky was acting like a good boy right now, but who knew how he would react in the car.

The three of us climbed into Vance's truck. Rocky, jumping right in and sitting on the back bench seat as if he rode in a pickup truck every day. He sat with his wings tucked in and his tail wrapped around his paws, panting with excitement.

I shook my head and mumbled "Twilight zone," as I buckled my seatbelt.

"What's that?" Vance asked as he pulled out of the parking lot.

"Twilight zone," I said on an exhale and proceeded to fill Vance in on everything happening around town, including Percy's odd behavior.

I finished the story about the time we rounded the lake, and everything fell eerily quiet. The fire truck had moved on, we didn't see any man-eating spiders, and even Rocky's counterpart was missing in action from the stoplight.

"Where to?" Vance asked me.

Something about Vance's remark reminded me about his evening plans. "Don't you have someplace to be?" I didn't mean to sound bitter, but even I could hear it in my voice.

Vance raised his eyebrows.

"Luke told me you were going out with Sally tonight."

"I see, and what's with the attitude?"

"I'm not giving you attitude," I lied.

Vance pulled over to the side of the road, gravel spraying out from under his tires as he abruptly came to a stop. Jamming the truck into park, he turned his full attention on me.

I tried not to shrink from his gaze, but it was hard. Vance was angry, I could see it in his eyes. His pupils flared, and I could swear he was counting until ten before speaking.

Or maybe it was thirty because the seconds ticked by, and he still didn't speak.

"Vance?" I asked hesitantly after I could no longer stand the silence.

"I asked you out. Remember? You said no. In fact, you made it abundantly clear that you didn't want a relationship with me."

"I know. I—"

Vance cut me off. "What am I supposed to do? Pine after you forever? Is that what you want?" Vance's eyes searched my face, and I felt cut open and raw by his scrutiny.

"No," I choked the word out. Even though inside, my mind screamed yes. Was that so much to ask? What was the matter with me? Vance was right. I told him that we were better off as friends. Yet the thought of him dating someone else sent my insides rolling. Was that it? Was I just jealous, and it was something I'd have to get over? Something I'd have to live with for the rest of my life? Or was it something more? And how did I know?

I wanted to tell Vance that I was sorry. That I didn't even understand my feelings, so how could I expect him to? But I couldn't find the right words. That didn't mean I wasn't going to try. I opened my mouth to speak, but Vance beat me to it.

"Turns out, it doesn't matter what you said." Vance stared out the windshield. The anger rushed out of him, extinguishing the flame that had burned so bright moments ago, replacing the emotion with something entirely different. Something that looked an awful lot like regret. "Because I'm still stuck on you." Vance said the words to the darkness.

The air rushed out of my lungs in a whoosh. I wasn't sure if I wanted to cry or smile, or to whoop and holler. Vance was stuck on me, and I was stuck on him. Oh, the irony of it all. I would be mad this time not to confess my feelings. Vance deserved to know he wasn't alone, that I felt exactly the same.

"Vance, I—"

Rocky abruptly put his paws on the center console from the backseat and started barking madly, interrupting the moment. I clapped my hands over my ears.

Someone had set off orange and purple fireworks over at the campground. The explosion filled the sky and drove Rocky nuts. The gargoyle jumped around in the backseat, scratching at the doors and barking at the embers. The entire cab rocked back and forth. I hated to see what Rocky's claws were doing to the seats.

"Okay, boy, we're going." Vance put the truck into gear and eased off the road. "Where to?" Vance repeated the question from before.

I wanted to check in with Misty, but first, we needed to stop in at the hay maze to see how things were going there and catch up with Percy.

"Next stop, maze of horrors, got it."

I grimaced at Vance's remark, hoping that the moniker wouldn't fit.

SIX

When we got to Village Square, the parking lot was still packed. Whatever was going on around town hadn't scared off the tourists. If anything, it only seemed to liven the atmosphere.

"Looks like we found where everyone's at," Vance remarked.

I agreed and got out of the truck.

The chill I felt earlier was more pronounced. Humidity rolled in off the lake, mixing with the crisp air, forming a blanket of fog at our feet.

"Spooky," Vance said, shutting the door after Rocky jumped down.

We walked across the parking lot toward the maze where Mr. McCormick stood. Deputy Amber Reynolds was there too. She was the one girl I despised from my school days. Okay, so there were only seventeen people in my graduating class, but if there had been a hundred, she'd still be public enemy number one. The blonde bombshell and I were opposite in every way, a reality that she insisted on pointing out all throughout our formative years. The fact that she was now a deputy, and her father was the sheriff, enabling her to bully me with her badge, was somehow fitting. It also wasn't a good sign.

"What's with the gargoyle?" Amber asked.

Rocky whimpered.

"Be nice. He's sensitive." Vance scratched Rocky's ears.

"Whatever." Amber then turned to me. "I'm not surprised to see you. Want to save us all the trouble and go on and confess?" Amber motioned to the maze behind her.

"Excuse me? I had nothing to do with this. I assume no one's come out yet?" I said the second part to Mr. McCormick.

The older man looked dead on his feet. The stress of the night was taking its toll on him. "No, and now Deputy Jones is lost too. I know you said not to allow anyone else in, but Amber insisted he check it out," Mr. McCormick apologized.

"He has a radio and a gun. If he was in trouble, we'd know." Amber rolled her eyes. "But if he doesn't come back, I'm blaming you," the irrational deputy rounded on me.

"What? That's absurd!" I shot back.

"Wasn't it your idea to have a hay maze in the first place?" Amber asked.

"I suggested it, but—" Amber cut me off.

"And didn't you convince Mr. McCormick to donate the hay?" she continued.

"Not really." I had assumed Mr. McCormick would supply the hay. He was the only man in town who sold it.

Amber ignored me. Rocky growled low in his throat. He didn't care for Amber either. The gargoyle was growing on me by the minute.

"Mr. McCormick said you even supplied the maze diagram," Amber continued.

"I supplied *a* diagram of a maze, which they didn't use." My maze paled in comparison to this architectural feat. I had very little to do with tonight's plans. The fall festival last month, yes. The Halloween Carnival, not so much. After the stress of the festival, I'd taken a much-needed reprieve from event planning.

"I'm sorry, Amber, but you really can't pin any of this on me. But I do think someone is out to ruin Halloween and Silverlake's reputation. The question is who?"

" I'm more worried about what's going on inside there than I am about who's responsible," Mr. McCormick referenced the maze once more.

"I agree. We need to get to the bottom of this,"

Vance looked at the forbidding hay structure once more.

"So, what do we do?" I envisioned tying a rope around my waist and heading in solo. Okay, maybe not solo. Vance could come too. I know he doesn't freeze up when things turn serious. But other than that, it would be the two of us heading in to investigate. If things got dicey, I could tug on the rope, and Mr. McCormick could pull us to safety. I relayed my plan to the group.

"I don't like it," Vance said before I was even done.

I started to protest, but Amber cut us both off. "As far as I'm concerned, there's no *we* here. You two are going to stand under that pecan tree over there while *I* figure this out."

"Now isn't the time for your ego," Vance chastised Amber.

"You think I'm going to let you two close enough to destroy any evidence? I'm watching you, like a hawk." Amber used her index and middle finger to point at her eyes before turning them to point toward us. "Now, go stand over there until I can deal with you. "

It took every bit of self-control not to curse Amber under my breath as I walked away. And by curse, I meant give her warts or a mustache, or maybe both if she kept it up.

Keeping my curses and thoughts to myself, I

walked over to the pecan tree Amber had pointed to and kept right on going. Vance wasn't surprised. "Bookstore?" he asked.

"Yup. Unless Amber's officially arresting or detaining me, I'm not listening to her. She has nothing on me, and we both know it. It's wishful thinking on her part."

"I'm going to walk down to the pet shop and get Rocky here a treat." Vance looked down at the gargoyle, who was now dancing at his feet. Apparently, the word treat was universal.

"You don't see Percy hovering around anywhere, do you?" I looked back over towards Mr. McCormick. Amber looked to be lecturing him with the way her hands were on her hips. It was probably about me and how this was all my fault, or some other gibberish. Unfortunately, that meant I couldn't ask Mr. McCormick about the roses, and I hadn't had a chance before Amber dismissed us.

"No, I don't." Vance scanned the crowd.

"Yeah, me either." I twisted my lips while I thought. Perhaps the next time Percy reappeared, we could walk over and talk to Mr. McCormick together. If Amber was still there, I was sure Percy could find a way to distract her.

"You know where to find me." Vance motioned for Rocky to follow him, which he willingly complied.

Vance and I parted ways, and I made a beeline for the bookstore before disaster could strike once more.

"Where have you been?" Misty greeted me at the door and shoved a tray in my hand.

"Putting out fires."

"Literally?"

"Not yet, but nothing would surprise me at this point."

"You can fill me in after helping me pick up these empty cups."

I was going to remind Misty it had been her idea to serve pumpkin punch. Clear cups, half-filled with orange juice, littered the place. I found them on end tables, book displays, and the floor next to abandoned chairs where they were just waiting to be kicked over.

"Pixies? Gargoyles? No wonder you've been missing in action," Misty said as we cleaned up her bookstore.

"I did call," I pointed out, but I never did send that text.

The small bookshop was packed. It was an older crowd with less little kids and more teenagers and adults looking for a more mature way to celebrate the holiday. Misty had set up a spooky photo station complete with ghosts in a graveyard background and several props for guests to pose with and take selfies. Upstairs, people mingled and browsed books at the same time. The mystery and horror sections being the most popular.

I noticed the snack table was picked over and even the punch bowl was almost empty. In terms of desserts, only a few cupcakes remained.

"I'm going to snag one of those before it's too late. I'm starving." Misty reached beside me and took one of Diane's cupcakes from La Luna bakery. It was a chocolate cupcake with fluffy white frosting and a candy pumpkin on top. I was about to copy Misty when someone called my name.

"Angelica, is that you, dear?" Mrs. Potts asked. Mrs. Potts had been my second-grade teacher, and tonight she was dressed up like a teapot, proving once and for all she had the best sense of humor.

"Mrs. Potts. How are you? I love your costume."

"Why thank you," she adjusted the lid-like hat on the top of her head. "I just wanted to thank you once again for recommending that cookbook. The Simmering Sisters can't get enough."

"Oh, I'm so happy to hear it." Mrs. Potts had stopped in when I was watching the store for Misty, looking for the perfect recipe for her cooking club. It was sheer luck I had been able to steer her in the right direction.

"Loretta Johnson can't even complain." My old teacher put her hand on her hip and poured herself out like in the song, I'm a Little Teapot.

"Now, that's impressive." Loretta Johnson

complained about everyone and everything. She was even more of a busybody than Mayor Parrish.

"I'm thinking of trying the double chocolate caramel bars next. They're said to cause nirvana." Mrs. Potts bounced her eyebrows. The recipes found in witchs' cookbooks were truly magical. Pot roast that left you fully satisfied, cupcakes that made you feel like a million bucks, tarts that could make you fall in love, and apparently Nirvana-inducing caramel bars. They were all par for the course.

"Now those I'd like to try." Who couldn't use a little Nirvana in their life?

Clemmie joined us at that moment looking a bit ragged, but who could blame her after the night she'd had. "I could use one of those caramel bars right about now," she said to Mrs. Potts.

"Angelica found the recipe." Mrs. Potts gave me all the credit.

"That doesn't surprise me. What would we do without you?" Clemmie was genuine in her praise.

"How's the shop?" I asked.

"I decided to lock up and deal with it tomorrow. I am too tired for all this hocus-pocus. Thought I would stop in for a minute and see if you'd heard anything on the pixies."

"Rogue pixies," I explained to Mrs. Potts.

"My word. It's been quite a night, hasn't it?" Mrs. Potts remarked.

"That it has," I agreed.

Misty threw her cupcake wrapper in the trash at the end of the table and joined our conversation. "Sorry to hear about the pixies," she said to Clemmie. "Hope they catch the RIBBIT." Misty's hand smacked her mouth. "PLUNK, PLUNK, RIBBIT," Misty tried again.

"What was that, dear?" Mrs. Potts leaned forward, thinking that it was only her that couldn't understand Misty.

"Not you too," Clemmie looked horrified.

"Aunt Thelma started croaking earlier today," I told Mrs. Potts.

"Croaking? My word!" Her eyes went wide.

I then looked to Misty, the dessert table, and back to Misty. Part of the puzzle clicked into place. "I think it's the cupcakes."

"The cupcakes?" Mrs. Pott's eyed the dessert table suspiciously.

"Remember? Aunt Thelma stopped at the bakery too." My comment was directed to Misty. "She had a bag from La Luna, and knowing Aunt Thelma, she would've eaten one cupcake at the bakery and taken one for the road."

"Now, who would go and curse a cupcake? What is wrong with people these days?" Clemmie tsked.

"I don't know, but we need to find out," I replied. Unfortunately, the store was packed.

I turned to Mrs. Potts. "Don't worry, I'll help keep

an eye on things here," she said before I could even ask.

"Thank you. We'll be back as soon as we can," I patted my second-grade teacher on the hand and quickly found Vicki, one of Misty's co-workers, and filled her in before our trio disappeared out the door.

SEVEN

We power walked from the bookstore to the bakery. My red cape billowed behind me. I gripped the loose fabric with my fist. The once cool breeze now felt unseasonably cold.

Along the way, we ran into Vance. Rocky had drawn a crowd. Both little kids and adults couldn't get enough of the gargoyle who was sporting a bright orange harness and leash. It was a good thing there weren't any mortals in town tonight, and we'd know if there were. Regular humans glowed. As in, their whole body lit up, making them easy to spot so we could keep our magic out of sight. Unlike Rocky. He was impossible to hide, and I didn't think any mortal would believe he was a dog in a costume, especially with the glowing red eyes.

"Diane's cupcakes have been cursed. Heading to

the bakery," I said in passing. Vance gave me a head nod that told me he'd understood.

La Luna wasn't as packed as The Candy Cauldron, but it was still busy. Little ghosts and goblins munched on frosted sugar cookies, bite-sized pumpkin pie tarts, and the suspected cursed cupcakes.

"Stop, step away from that cupcake," Clemmie said to a little boy dressed as a firefighter. The boy replied by shoving the whole thing in his mouth. Frosting and crumbs stuck to his face.

"Why, you! Kids these days just don't listen," Clemmie said to no one in particular.

The little boy's mom ushered her son back to the table, side eying Clemmie the whole time.

"What's wrong?" Diane moved away from helping customers, letting her co-worker take over, and ushered us forward.

We cut to the front of the line, and I whispered over the counter, "We think the cupcakes might be cursed. Aunt Thelma ate one and so did Misty, and now they can't stop croaking."

"It happened right after she ate it," Clemmie added.

"RIBBIT," Misty opened her mouth and added her two cents. Then, from behind us, the little firefighter croaked.

Diane looked aghast, "Who would do such a thing?"

"I don't know, but that's not all that's going on." I explained to Diane the chaos happening around town.

We watched Mayor Parrish walk by the front window, looking rather smug. Her nose high in the air. If it started to rain, she'd drown.

"I bet it's her. You know how much she hates all this." Diane motioned to the costumes and decorations.

"I know, but do you really think she'd sabotage her own town's Halloween?" I asked.

Diane looked to Clemmie before they both said, "Yep."

"PLUNK," added Misty in agreement.

I sighed. Even I had to agree that Mayor Parrish was probably to blame. The mayor stopped outside the bakery where Diane had set a bowl of candy out for tick-or-treaters. Mayor Parrish picked up a fun size candy bar, examined the package, wrinkled her nose, and dropped it unceremoniously back in the bowl. "You're right. I bet it is her."

"If she could've cancelled Halloween, she would've." Diane's voice held a hint of sadness.

"Maybe this is her attempt at trying." Clemmie folded her arms across her chest.

"How are we going to prove it?" Diane asked.

"Leave that to me," I replied. Not many witches could transform into animals. It was a trait passed down from one's mother to the oldest child. My mother had been able to do it, and hence, the gift had been passed down to me. My tiger eye pendant grew warm against my chest. The circular pendant housed a round, spinning gemstone that dangled on a gold chain. The stone provided protection, courage, strength, and something extra magical. It gave me, and only me, the power to transfigure into a cat. Holding on to the tiger stone around my neck, I closed my eyes and prepared to say the incantation that would transform me to my feline alter ego: Metamorfóno alithís ousía.

But before I could speak the words, in walked Mayor Parrish herself.

I'm not one to usually be rendered speechless. In fact, I pride myself on having a level head. But at that moment, words failed me.

Thankfully, Mayor Parish was too focused on her task at hand to notice how guilty the four of us looked standing there. She walked past us and met up with some customers in the bakery who were enjoying their sweet treats. Always a politician, the mayor put on the fakest smile ever and asked the customers how they were enjoying their evening. From how she raved about the decorations and turnout, you would think she invented Halloween herself, but I knew better. It was all a show.

What I wasn't expecting though was for Mayor Parrish to sink her teeth into one of Diane's cursed cupcakes. A customer offered her the one that she had just bought, and Mayor Parrish readily accepted. None of us were quick enough to stop her, or maybe it was morbid curiosity to see what would happen next.

The curse didn't disappoint.

Within seconds of swallowing, Mayor Parrish opened her mouth and let out an unexpected croak.

"CROAK, RIBBIT, RIBBIT!" The mayor looked gobsmacked, croaking and ribbiting around the bakery.

"This means it's not her, right?" Clemmie asked.

"Not unless she wants to throw us off the scent," I remarked, but as I saw the mayor frantically waving her arms around with a chorus of frog sounds coming out of her mouth, I rethought that statement. Mayor Parrish wouldn't willingly make a fool out of herself, and that was exactly what she was doing. Customers, open-mouthed, stared at the spectacle.

The mayor rounded on Diane and pointed an accusatory finger at her chest.

Diane held her arms up in surrender. "Don't look at me. I didn't do it. No way would I jeopardize my business with some silly Halloween curse." Before the mayor could utter another ribbit, Diane turned to me. "Listen, I've been selling cupcakes all night, and not everyone's left here croaking."

"What do you think it is then?" Clemmie asked.

"I don't know," Diane confessed.

We were silent for a moment. Mayor Parrish took

out her wand and attempted to un-spell herself, tapping her wrist with her wand tip repeatedly, like a conductor tapping his baton on the podium to get the orchestra's attention.

"She better watch herself," Clemmie warned and leaned back just in time. Green sparks flew out of Mayor Parish's wand followed by a puff of orange smoke. The lot of us coughed and waved our hand to clear the air.

When the smoke dissipated, the mayor turned to face us. Her hair was blown back, and toad-like warts covered her face.

My mouth dropped open in shock.

Diane's hand covered her mouth.

Clemmie snorted. "Nuh-uh, that does not look good."

Mayor Parish ran her hand down her face, seeming to check herself out. Feeling the bumps, she promptly dashed to the bathroom. A string of croaks and plunks trailed after her. The customer who had given her the cupcake ran after her.

Our group got back to solving the mystery.

"Which cupcake did you eat?" Diane asked Misty. Misty pointed to the chocolate cupcake with white frosting and a sugared pumpkin on top. "The same one I sold your aunt and the one that Mayor Parrish just ate," Diane added.

"Did you make everything yourself?" I asked.

"I did. Fresh this morning. Even whipped up the

icing back here in the kitchen." Diane thought for a minute before adding, "Well, everything but the candy pumpkins. I picked those up this afternoon from The Candy Cauldron."

"The Candy Cauldron?" I immediately thought of Beatrice and Sabrina playing in Luke's kitchen. The twins were definitely mischievous enough to curse a batch of candy, and they would think a frog curse would be hilarious. What kid wouldn't? "I think I know who's to blame, and I don't think they meant any harm. Grab those candy pumpkins and follow me."

The Candy Cauldron was still busy, although things had calmed down a bit. By that, I mean there were only three people in line rather than the line being out the door. Beatrice and Sabrina had moved to help their uncle behind the counter. I smiled at the twins when we entered the store, but one look at the bagged candy pumpkins in my hand had both girls retreating back to the kitchen.

"Hold on," I said to the girls.

"We didn't mean any harm. It was a joke. We thought it would be fun. A trick and a treat rolled together." The girls talked so fast it was hard to tell who said what.

"What's going on here?" Luke joined us at the end of the counter.

"Your nieces were having a bit of fun. It looks like they cursed these candies that Diane put on her cupcakes. Now, several people are out there croaking like frogs," I said.

"You guys did what?" Luke was shocked. "You promised me you wouldn't do that again. You have to tell people before you curse their candy."

"Again?" Clemmie asked.

"Last time, I barked like a dog for a week."

"These don't last as long." Sabrina shook her head encouragingly.

"Just a day or two," Beatrice added.

"A day or two? Now, that's not right," Clemmie said.

Misty's eyes were wide in alarm.

"Girls." Luke admonished his nieces. "You can't curse people without them knowing. If they find out the candy came from here and not to mention Diane's bakery, people might not want to shop here anymore. We could go out of business." Luke looked at his nieces with disappointment. "Plus, do you remember what Sheriff Reynolds told you?" Luke cocked his head.

"That it's illegal." The girls said together, their shoulders drooping.

"But it wasn't a serious curse," Sabrina interjected, trying to rationalize her behavior.

"You want to tell that to the sheriff?" Luke asked.

Sabrina opened her mouth and then shut it. For the first time, the little girl was at a loss for words. It was Beatrice that spoke. "I'm sorry, we didn't think of it that way."

"Honest." Sabrina looked up with tears in her eyes.

My heart hurt for the girls. I knew they hadn't meant any harm. I was going to say as much when Sabrina said, "Wait, we can fix it!"

"We can?" Beatrice said to her sister at the same time Luke said, "How?"

"We can make counter-curse chocolates and pass them out as free samples. Everyone can have one!" Sabrina said.

"That's a great idea!" Beatrice exclaimed. "Can we, uncle?"

"We'll tell everyone it's our fault." Sabrina looked somber.

"And promise to never curse candy again," Beatrice added.

Sabrina started to object to that promise. Beatrice elbowed her sister. Hard in the ribs. "Right. Promise." Sabrina rubbed her side.

"So, can we get to work in the kitchen?" Beatrice asked.

Luke sighed, and the girls knew they had him. "It's probably the only option we've got."

The girls turned on their heels, but Clemmie stopped them. "What about everything else going on around town? You didn't set those pixies free in my store, did you?" Clemmie looked rather cross.

"Pixies? We don't have any pixies," Beatrice said.

"I don't even like pixies. They're creepy," Sabrina said.

"We've been here the whole time. The only thing we did was curse the candy."

"Promise."

The girls nodded their heads together in unison to add more weight to their story.

No one said anything for a minute.

Diane spoke first. "I think they are telling the truth."

"I think they are too," I agreed.

Clemmie shrugged her shoulders. I could tell she wanted answers, but she wasn't going to get them out of the twins.

"Can we get to work Uncle Luke?" Sabrina asked.

Luke nodded his approval before turning to us. "I'm sorry about all of this. If I hadn't been so busy and we weren't short staffed..."

"Those nieces of yours will keep you on your toes," Clemmie said, still a bit peeved.

"It's okay, Luke. It's not your fault. We'll let you get back to work."

Luke nodded his thanks.

EIGHT

When we left The Candy Cauldron, Misty was no longer croaking. We had waited around while Luke supervised the girls making the counter-curse chocolates. Misty sampled the first chocolate, and it worked like magic. The twins were currently running around Village Square passing chocolates out to everyone they could get to take one.

"Compliments of The Candy Cauldron," Sabrina shouted.

"Enjoy! Happy Halloween!" Beatrice exclaimed over her shoulder.

"I have to get back to the bookstore, but keep me posted," Misty said, waving goodbye before trailing after the girls.

Our trio stood off to the side while we attempted to figure this case out.

"Well, at least we know who's cursing the

cupcakes," Diane said with relief. She had her own bag of counter-cursed chocolates in her hand for the bakery.

"I'm not worried about the cupcakes. I want to know who's responsible for destroying my store," Clemmie interjected.

I had to agree with Clemmie there. While it was nice to know who was behind the cupcakes, I too wanted to know who was out to ruin Halloween. I was usually good at coming up with suspects, but I was drawing a blank right then.

Then again, what if we had been right all along?

"You know, if the twins are only responsible for the cupcakes, that means Mayor Parrish could still be behind the rest of the chaos."

Clemmie clapped her hands together. "You're right, she could be. Where do you think she's run off to now? I say we hunt her down and make her spill the beans."

"I don't know about spilling the beans, but we do have to find her. Maybe we can catch her in the act, round up some sort of evidence." We would need something more than our word against the mayor's. Our friends would believe us, but that wouldn't get us very far with the sheriff or his daughter.

"She's probably still locked in the bakery's bathroom," Diane remarked.

"If I looked like her, I'd lock myself in the bathroom, too," Clemmie quipped.

"Guess let's find out." We headed back around the curvy, cobblestoned path to the bakery. I eyed the hay maze in passing, but nothing remarkable seemed to be happening. I wasn't sure if that was a good thing or not. Fog continued to build and condense around the maze. It was odd the way it pooled there, like a thick blanket. It was almost as if Mr. McCormick and Molly had added dry ice to the fountain in the middle for effect. I supposed I couldn't rule that out, although the fog seemed to be growing thicker by the minute.

"Mayor Parrish still here?" Diane asked one of her workers, Anna, when we walked in.

"Oh, no. She glamoured her face and left in a huff," Anna replied.

"Well, if she comes back, call me on my cell phone. In the meantime, if anyone comes in croaking, give them one of these." The young witch took the bag from Diane. "And explain a couple of kids pulled a prank, but rest assured, everything here is safe and delicious. Feel free to dole out a free sample or two. Can't be too giving when it comes to damage control."

"Okay." Anna looked less sure. "Oh, but I did tell the mayor about the candy, or what you guys suspected. I think she was heading to The Candy Cauldron next."

"You've got to be kidding me," Clemmie looked back out the door.

"We must have passed her," Diane said.

"It wouldn't surprise me." With the crowded and darkened streets, anything was possible.

"You're telling me we're going back to The Candy Cauldron? Didn't we just come from there?" I had to agree, we were traipsing all over Village Square and getting nowhere. "It's a good thing I wore my tennis shoes today," Clemmie grumbled.

"You and me both," I said with a half-smile.

"I'll be back in time to close," Diane said to Anna as we walked out. "And if you see the mayor, call me."

"And tell her to stay put!" Clemmie added.

Anna waved goodbye, and we filed back out.

In less than ten minutes, we were back at The Candy Cauldron.

Luke looked weary when we trooped back into his shop, which was empty for once. "Mind flipping the sign to closed?"

"Consider it done." Clemmie had the sign turned and the door locked within seconds.

I looked at the clock on the wall, surprised to see Luke closing a bit early. "Calling it a day?"

"It's not worth the stress. I need a break. Plus, we're just about sold out of everything." Luke motioned to his mostly empty display case. Even the saltwater taffy in the window looked stretched to within an inch of its life.

"We keep drawing in these types of crowds, we're going to have to start hiring Halloween help,"

Diane remarked. Clemmie and Luke nodded in agreement.

"Did Mayor Parrish stop by?" I asked.

"What do you think?" I suddenly knew why Luke looked so beat. "My only saving grace was there were customers here. Even then, she still tore into me and the shop, threatening legal action. Thankfully, a couple regulars spoke up. They thought the chocolates were in good fun, and the mayor needed to lighten up."

"Bet she didn't take that too well," Clemmie chimed in.

"She left right after, but not before saying her lawyer would be in touch," Luke remarked looking defeated.

"If you ask me, the mayor might need a little memory manipulation," Clemmie said under her breath to me.

"Don't you dare. It's illegal," I hissed. A witch could alter a mortal's memory (especially if it was to keep our secrets safe), but you couldn't go around scrambling everyone's neurons just for the heck of it.

"Just sayin'," Clemmie shrugged. "Not like I don't know a good lawyer."

"Leave Vance out of this." I honestly wouldn't put it past Clemmie to erase the mayor's memory. I wasn't sure if I should be amused or alarmed at her suggestion.

"Any idea where she went to after here?" Diane asked.

"Not a clue, but I'm headed home before she can come back." I didn't blame Luke one bit.

"What did you find out?" Vance and Rocky joined us as we stepped back outside. The gargoyle looked content as could be next to Vance's side if his lolling tongue and goofy grin were any indication.

"That the twins cursed the cupcakes, or the candy that was on top of them anyway," I said.

"And Mayor Parrish is still our bad guy," Clemmie said.

"Are you sure?" Vance asked.

"Well, she's the only suspect we can think of," Diane looked around the group to confirm she was right.

We nodded.

"I can't think of anyone else," I agreed.

Vance's brow furrowed. "We better head to the cafe then. I just saw the mayor head inside."

"Mayor Prissy Pants better not do anything to the cafe," Clemmie said.

"Let her try." Vance's mom, Heather, owned the cafe. Heather could hold her own, but her son wouldn't let her face a threat alone. Vance withdrew his wand from his pocket. Rocky growled at his side. For Mayor Parrish's sake, I hoped she wasn't up to something fishy.

The cafe was next door to the bookstore. On a

typical day, I loved to grab lunch from the cafe and sit outside the bookstore with a good book, but nothing about tonight was normal. A chill traveled up my spine when I stepped inside the restaurant. I looked over my shoulder to gauge where the feeling had originated from. My eyes locked with Amber. I swear I felt like sticking my tongue out at the deputy. It was ridiculous how immature the woman made me act. Amber walked into the cafe behind us. I tried to ignore her. After all, we had a mayor to hunt down.

"I thought I told you to wait for me by that tree," Amber snapped at me.

"Last I checked, I wasn't under arrest." With the intonation of my voice, I might as well have added na-na na-na boo-boo after it.

"You still should have waited."

"Waiting under that tree wouldn't have done any of us any good. I'm trying to find out what's going on too. Trying to help you," I clarified. "You could make both of our lives easier if you'd accept that."

"I'll do no such thing. You think you're so smart, waltzing in here, solving crimes. You might have the rest of this town under your spell, but I'm watching you."

While I continued to go back-and-forth with Amber, Vance inquired after his mom's whereabouts. "Where did they go?" Vance's voice held an edge to it.

I turned away from Amber. "What's wrong?"

"Betty says she saw the mayor talking to my mom

back here in the hallway, and she hasn't seen either one of them since."

"Where did they go?" I repeated Vance's question to the waitress.

"I don't know. I was busy with my tables." Betty looked around the restaurant for Heather and shook her head as if she didn't have a clue.

"I'll check the bathrooms," Clemmie said.

"I'll go look in the kitchen," Vance replied.

"I'll head out front. Maybe they slipped outside, and nobody saw them," Diane offered.

"What's going on?" Amber asked.

"Have you seen Mayor Parrish?" I replied.

"No, some of us have been busy working. Why?"

I was careful in my response, not wanting to tip the deputy off with our suspicions. "She has her thumb on the pulse of this town. She might be able to help solve tonight's mystery."

"Oh, well... No, I haven't."

I turned away from Amber and left her to her own thoughts. If she was any sort of deputy, she'd put two and two together and start looking for the mayor herself, but I wasn't holding my breath.

I copied Diane's suggestion and walked out front, turning to the right and walking down the sidewalk. I spotted Diane behind me, walking in the opposite direction. A small alleyway separated the cafe from the bookstore. Because of the layout of the shops, trash receptacles and dumpsters were kept on the side of buildings as opposed to behind them. Most of the shops had fountains or gardens that ran behind them in addition to walkways, or seating areas, like the bookstore had. The cafe's outdoor dining area was in front, while the bookstore's was in the back.

I followed my intuition and snuck into the alleyway.

Mayor Parrish's voice echoed off the brick wall. "Just this way. A little further," the mayor coaxed her unwilling companion.

"I don't see anything," came Heather's voice.

"Trust me," the mayor replied.

I didn't trust that woman any further than I could throw her.

With my back pressed against the wall, I moved slowly, while listening intently.

"Don't mind the darkness. Your eyes will adjust," Mayor Parrish said.

At that remark, I did two things simultaneously. I took out my wand and my cell phone. As quietly as possible, I turned on the video recording function on my phone. I needed hard proof that Mayor Parrish was behind the wrongdoings tonight. Video evidence was the best chance I had. But I wasn't going to let her hurt Heather either. I had to be prepared to act, which is where my wand came into play.

"Down here, by the dumpster. That's it, just a little further. You have to get down real close to the ground," Mayor Parrish continued.

I wondered what the mayor was playing at. Was she going to throw Heather into a dumpster or curse her behind one?

"I'm sorry, I have to get back." Heather stepped back from the mayor.

In the darkness, the mayor grabbed Heather by her wrist and pulled her forward. "No, you must stay."

"The cafe's busy. They need me."

"No, look." The mayor yanked Heather down to the ground behind the dumpster and out of my view.

That was it, I sprang into action, sprinting the fifty yards that separated us. Wand out, I was ready to make the mayor spit ice cubes. Glacio was, in fact, one of my favorite spells.

"Oh, they're adorable," Heather cooed. I slid to a stop, wand raised above my head like a witch ready to strike.

"Good heavens, Angelica." Mayor Parrish slapped her hand over her heart. "What on earth are you doing?"

"What am I doing? What are you doing dragging Heather down a dark alley?"

"Nothing nefarious, I promise you. My word. Look for yourself." Nestled behind the dumpster were four little black fluff balls. "I need Heather's help feeding these kittens. The mother's under here somewhere. I was trying to coax her out."

"ROWR," came the most pitiful meow from under the dumpster.

I lowered my wand. "I might know the mom. A black cat stopped in at the bookstore this afternoon when I was decorating."

At that moment, I did what any good witch does when she finds a cat hiding under a dumpster. I got down on my hands and knees and pleaded with the kitty to come out.

"Here, kitty, kitty. Come out, sweetheart. Are you hungry? Do you want something to eat?" I followed it up with kissing noises. The mama cat replied with another pitiful meow. Heather had already back-tracked to the cafe and was back within a minute, some freshly shredded chicken at hand. Heather set the container down. The kittens were too young to eat it, but that didn't mean they didn't want to try. Mayor Parrish scooped a kitten up in each hand. Heather did the same, holding the kittens to her chest.

"Yowch, you've got some sharp nails," Heather remarked as the kittens clawed through her black sweater.

I took a couple pieces of the chicken and tossed them under the dumpster and closer to the mama. Two yellow eyes reflected back at me. I watched as the cat cautiously sniffed the chicken before eventually taking a nibble. The cat must not have been entirely feral because, within minutes, it came out from behind the dumpster and was ready for a second helping. I let the cat have free rein of the bowl. She scarfed down the meal.

"Now, what should we do with these guys?" I asked.

"I can't keep them at the cafe, but I can give you some more chicken," Heather said.

"I don't want to leave them here. But as mayor, duty calls. I can't very well disappear with a litter of kittens on tonight of all nights."

Both Heather and Mayor Parrish looked to me. "I suppose I can see if Misty can keep them at the bookstore until I'm ready to go home." I wasn't sure what I was going to do with a litter of kittens, either, but I could take care of them for a few days until we figured that out. "Do you have a box?" I asked Heather. If not, I could sprint back to the pet store, but I was really tired of running all over Village Square.

"I'm sure I have something. I'll be right back." Heather handed me her two kittens and jogged back to the cafe.

"You know," Mayor Parrish said when it was just the two of us. "I think we can give Harrisville a run for its money." I knew what the mayor meant. Before the chaos kicked off, Silverlake had really outdone itself. "That is if we don't scare away all the tourists tonight."

"I thought you didn't like all of this Halloween mumbo jumbo."

"Well, a person has a right to change her mind. And, it appears I have been overruled."

Heather came back with the box, interrupting our conversation. Even though it was chilly, I unfastened my cloak and used it to line the box. We tucked the kittens safely inside first. Shockingly, the mama cat climbed in the box too. A chorus of purrs filled the alley.

"Now, I need to figure out what's going on with that maze once and for all," Mayor Parrish announced.

"Let me talk with Misty," I referenced the large box between my arms, "and then I'll meet you over there."

Vance looked ready to lose it when he spotted us walk out of the alley. But it was Rocky who lurched forward. His animal instincts were on point. The gargoyle was curious to know what I was carrying in the box. "They're kittens. Mayor Parrish wanted your mom to help her get them out from behind the dumpster. I'm going to see if Misty can keep them at the bookstore and then head over to the maze."

I did just that while Heather talked to her son and tried to calm him down.

NINE

"I'm almost scared to ask," Misty said as I walked in. My red velvet cloak dangled over the box's edge.

"They're kittens. A mama cat, too. Do you mind if I keep them here in the back until I'm ready to go home?"

"You want to keep a box of kittens in a bookstore?" Misty looked at me like I was a bit nutty.

"It'll be for less than an hour. I'll put them in your office. Under the desk. I'm sure they'll be perfect little angels."

Misty looked at me like she didn't believe that for a second. "Fine, but you will be cleaning up any accidents they have. And believe me, there will be accidents." Misty gave me a look that said, know what I'm saying?

I hadn't considered the whole litter box situation.

I had better help figure out the maze and solve this case fast.

"Hey, I meant to ask you, what happened with the caramel apples and pumpkin truffles?" Misty asked as we tucked the kitchen safely in their box under her desk.

"What do you mean?" I stood up.

"Where did they go? I sent you off to pick them up and never saw them."

"I gave them to a vampire."

"A real vampire?"

"No, thank heavens. There was a guy coming into the bookstore. He said he was going to your party. I asked him to give them to you."

Misty shook her head no.

"No?" I repeated.

"I never saw him or the treats."

"Well, that's odd. Maybe he decided to keep them all for himself?" It was really the only thing I could think of. What a single vampire would do with a couple dozen apples and pumpkin truffles was beyond me. "I guess I'll keep an eye out for him. In the meantime, I'm going to meet Mayor Parrish back at the maze."

"You two are working together now?"

"Trust me, I'm just as surprised as you are."

If I thought the fog was thick before, it was nothing to how it was outside now. I could barely see my hand in front of my face, let alone the maze entrance. Vance was waiting for me under the pecan tree that Amber originally asked us to stay by. He let out a big yawn that mirrored how I felt.

"Yeah, it's been a long night," I remarked.

"I swear I was wide awake two minutes ago," Vance confessed.

"Well, I wasn't," I laughed and then copied Vance's yawn. But even I had to admit my fatigue had gotten exponentially worse since coming closer to the maze.

"Is Mayor Parrish here?" I asked.

"I think so. It's hard to make out who's who." Vance yawned again.

I leaned my head back against the tree and felt like closing my eyes and resting. Just a five-minute nap. I was sure that was all I needed. Rocky barked and jostled me awake.

"What in the heck is going on?" My eyelids fought to stay open.

"Hmmm?" Vance said. His eyes were closing too.

"Wake up." I swatted Vance's arm.

"Huh, what?"

"Why are we so tired?" Even as I asked, I yawned again. I had to fight the urge to rest my head back against the tree.

Rocky barked two more times. The booming sound helped clear my head. "Vance, wake up." He had fallen asleep against the tree. "Vance, come on. You have to wake up."

"Just five more minutes, Mom."

A breeze blew more of the fog my way and my eyelids fluttered shut. "You're right. Five minutes. That's all we need." It was sad how easily I fell to Vance's suggestion. The fog pulled at me. I wanted to cave into it so badly. Rocky licked my hand. The sensation brought me back to my senses. Somehow the gargoyle was impervious to the fog.

"Come on, Vance, walk with me." The fog swallowed my words. I felt like I was walking through water. My body was just so tired. It took a Herculean effort to get close to the maze, and when I did, I saw that Mr. McCormick and Mayor Parrish were snoozing soundly on bales of hay.

I jostled Mr. McCormick. "Hey, wake up." The council member snorted a couple times before soft snores took back over.

I tried the mayor instead. "Mayor Parrish. Wake up," I clapped my hands, but they sounded weak to my ears. Like I was clapping with a pair of wool mittens on.

Rocky came up behind us and barked his thunderous warning. The noise worked wonders.

"Molly?" Mr. McCormick mumbled his daughter's name as he came to.

"I'm here! Duty calls. Mayor Parrish is here," the mayor woke with a start.

"Guys, listen, it's the fog. It's making everyone sleepy. We have to get away from it." No sooner were the words out of my mouth did I yawn. The hay bales did look awfully comfortable.

"What? What are you talking about?" Mayor Parrish closed her eyes. She would be back to snoozing in another second. Rocky tugged on her pant leg. Mayor Parrish looked down through half-closed lids. Seeing that it was a gargoyle, she let out a shriek. "Help! It's a beast. A horrible beast!"

Rocky's tail wagged back and forth.

"He's not a beast," I awkwardly patted Rocky's head seeing my arm felt like it was asleep.

Beside me Mr. McCormick tried to stand up, but his balance was off. The poor man was dead on his feet. Rocky walked over to his side to help stabilize him. I didn't know where Vance was. I assumed he was back sleeping by the tree.

"We need to get away from the fog," I reiterated. "C'mon, follow me." I shuffled forward, away from the maze. I told myself to just keep walking. I focused on lifting one foot after the other. With each step, my footsteps became lighter. My eyelids no longer felt heavy. The air became crisp and clear.

"Well, that was the strangest thing." Mayor Parrish looked back to the maze once we were in the clear.

"Someone's bewitched it. I bet everyone inside is asleep," I said.

"We need to tear it down. Get rid of it," Mayor Parrish insisted.

"What we need to do is get everyone out," Vance said, coming up behind us, Rocky at his side. The gargoyle must've gone back for him. And I thought dogs were man's best friend. Vance rubbed the sleep from his eyes.

"Anyone have any ideas?" I asked.

"We could try to blow it away with a wind spell," Mayor Parrish suggested.

"That's not a bad idea." Although, given how thick the fog was, we'd need a community effort to dissipate it.

"It's too thick. That will take too long," Vance replied, reading my thoughts.

"But if we don't act fast, all of Silverlake will be deep asleep," Mr. McCormick said.

"What are we going to do? I can't let my constituents fall asleep! This will be the worst Halloween ever, and it's on my watch!" Mayor Parrish's voice turned shrill.

"Calm down. Let's think. How can we rescue everyone?" I asked.

"Can this guy get everyone out?" Mr. McCormick pointed down to Rocky.

"He could try." Vance looked skeptical. Rocky cocked his head to the side, mirroring Vance's expression.

I knew what Vance was thinking. Rocky was a good boy, but we needed something on a larger scale. Call in the cavalry, so to speak. "Wait a minute, that's it. I think I know what to do. Mayor Parrish, call Fire Chief Grady and get the fire department here. They have oxygen tanks they can wear. That way they won't breathe in the fog."

"And they'll be able to pull everyone out of the maze," Mayor Parrish filled in.

"The fog is just like smoke," Mr. McCormick said.

"Exactly. They're the most qualified. Then once everyone is out, we can figure out how to get rid of the fog."

"And arrest the culprit. This foolishness has gone on for far too long," Mayor Parrish took out her cell phone. "Leave it to me," she said, and surprisingly, I knew I could.

TEN

The firetrucks rolled in within minutes. In no time, the firefighters were able to pull out the maze goers without a problem. Most of them looked like zombies, completely out of it, but once people got away from the fog, they came around.

Fire Chief Grady trailed after them, holding a chunk of neon purple glowing ice. "Sleep of the Dead, if I'm not mistaken."

"I'll take that," Deputy Amber said. She walked right up to the fire chief with an evidence bag in hand and proceeded to pass out stone cold. The fire chief dropped the ice and caught Amber by the arm as she swayed on her feet.

"No one ever said she was bright," I mumbled to Vance.

"Not like you," Vance replied.

"Gee, you're just now noticing?" I joked. "But still,

I'm not smart enough. I don't know who's behind all this." I couldn't keep the frustration from my voice. "You didn't by chance see a middle-aged vampire creeping around here, did you?"

"A vampire? In Silverlake?" Vance's eyes darted around the darkness in front of him.

"Not a real vampire. A guy dressed up in a costume. I gave him the candy apples for the bookstore, but Misty never saw them. Something doesn't add up."

"Was he a local?"

"That's the thing, I'm not sure. He seemed familiar, but it was hard to tell with the costume."

"No, but I'll definitely be walking you home tonight."

I changed the subject. I was an expert at that. "Anyway, speaking of being smart, I was going to grab one of the chocolates for Aunt Thelma for when I get home." I looked down at my phone. "The bakery is open for ten more minutes." They were open late for the holiday. I shot Diane a text to make sure she still had some chocolates left. She replied that she did, and she'd be on the lookout for me.

"I'll walk with you," Vance suggested.

I nodded and was ready to go when the fire chief joined us.

"Are you planning on keeping that gargoyle?" Chief Grady walked up and asked Vance.

"Uh, not sure." Vance looked down to Rocky who

replied with a playful yip. "Don't they turn back to stone when the sun comes up?"

"Not if they've been bewitched, or so I'm told," Chief Grady replied.

"Oh, well yeah, I guess so. If the church is okay with it and Rocky here wants to stay." The gargoyle danced at Vance's feet. The answer was clearly a yes.

Just then the second gargoyle appeared at the fire chief's feet and looked up at him adoringly. The Chief Grady absently rubbed his pointed ears. "I think these guys deserve some time off after guarding the town the last hundred or so years."

"I think you're right," Vance replied.

I interrupted the conversation by touching Vance's forearm. "I'm going to go grab that chocolate. I'll be right back." I left Vance and Grady to talk all things gargoyles and made my way to the bakery.

Things were finally winding down around Village Square, and what a night it had been. And somewhere down the line, Vance had adopted a gargoyle, and I was fostering a litter of kittens. I shook my head. I should learn by now to always expect the unexpected. I took a deep breath and tried to give myself a pep talk. It was okay that I didn't catch the Halloween Hijacker, as I was now dubbing him or her. Tomorrow was a new day, and perhaps a good night's sleep would do me wonders and help me unravel the clues. Mayor Parrish's spot as Suspect Number One was now replaced by the mysterious vampire. Who was he? He was a witch, that was for sure. Probably someone local. Not one of the shop owners. Not a teacher either. I'd seen him before, but not regularly.

Rustling in the bushes caught my attention. Instantly, I reached for my wand. I wasn't about to let someone ambush me. My heart rate accelerated and my palms turned sweaty.

"Angelica?" Mayor Parrish said from behind me.

I rounded on her. My wand pointed right at her chest.

The mayor put her hands up in surrender. "Good heavens, what are you doing? That's the second time you've drawn your wand on me tonight."

I lowered my wand. "Sorry, just on edge. I heard something behind that tree." I eyed the source of the noise one more time but didn't see anything.

"Oh well, I'm sure it's nothing. Anyway, I wanted to formally say thank you for your help tonight."

"Thank you?" Mayor Parrish was full of surprises tonight.

"Yes, without your help, I don't know what would've happened. Whenever there was a problem, you were there, helping to make it right."

"Yes-th, you sure were." The vampire came out of the bushes. Mayor Parrish cocked her head. The man continued to walk forward. Light from the store windows spilled onto the walkway, casting the man's face in relief.

"Gerald Blackworth, is that you?" Mayor Parrish leaned forward to see the man better.

"Gerald Blackworth, as in the mayor of Hendersonville?" I asked.

The mayor waved his cape and bowed. When he stood, his wand was outstretched, pointing at my face.

"Drop it," he commanded, pointing to my own wand. I did as I was told. "Into the alley." He motioned with the wand.

"What's the matter with you? And take out those teeth. You sound ridiculous," Mayor Parrish said, but moved toward the alley none the less.

Mayor Blackworth removed the teeth and threw them to the ground. "What is the matter with me? You and your town stealing Halloween is what's the matter!" he shouted.

"What are you talking about? Your town caters to mortals," Mayor Parrish said dismissively.

"Mortals? Where do you think witches celebrate Halloween? Hendersonville! Or they used to. This year you ruined everything. First, it was your fall festival, and now this! Tourism is already down twenty percent!"

"That hardly seems statistically relevant," Mayor Parrish said.

Mayor Blackworth fired a warning spell. Red sparks shot past our faces. "Stop talking."

"What are you going to do?" I looked into the darkened alley way.

Mayor Blackworth smiled. The image sent shivers down my spine. "First I'm going to erase your memory. Then, I'm going to fill it with hatred for Halloween. Make it so you never want to celebrate it ever again!" The man chuckled. He looked like a demented little vampire.

Unfortunately for him, that was not going to happen. I had enough of this man's games. I was done playing around. It was time to take action.

In the blink of an eye, I reached up for my tiger's eye. Before Mayor Blackworth could react, the spell had passed my lips, and I transformed into a cat, and with that, came my cat-like reflexes. My eyes instantly adjusted to the darkness and I could see Hendersonville's mayor clear as day.

It was almost too easy.

Mayor Blackworth was frozen in shock. He couldn't react as I sprang on him, literally jumping off his chest and stealing his wand with my teeth. My back nails dug into his chest as I sprang off and back onto the ground.

Mayor Parrish wasted no time, withdrawing her own wand and holding Mayor Blackworth in place. "Go ahead, make my Halloween," she threatened. I meowed my approval from the ground.

"Is everything okay?" Diane asked, peering into the alley. She quickly took in the scene.

"No, it's not okay. Mayor Blackworth was behind everything tonight. He wanted to erase our memories and take away Halloween." Mayor Parrish's voice was one level below shrieking.

"I'm calling the sheriff," Diane said, her phone out and held to her ear.

Meanwhile, I morphed back into human form. Mayor Blackworth looked like he wished he could transform into a bird and fly away. "Shall we try?" I asked, reading the expression on his face. "Maybe a toad instead. It would serve you right," I suggested.

Mayor Blackworth held his hands up higher. "Please don't, I'm sorry. I was only thinking of my town. A mayor would do anything for his citizens."

"Including breaking the law?" I raised my eyebrows in question.

"Tsk, tsk. It's a darn shame your constituents aren't witches. It would be easier to explain your arrest." Mayor Parish jabbed her wand in the air in his direction like a sword.

"M-M-M-My arrest?"

"Or we could set the townsfolk loose on you," I suggested.

Mayor Blackworth looked over his shoulder to the crowd that had gathered. Two sets of glowing red eyes glared back at him. Only we knew the gargoyles were friendly. "I-I-I... I'll never do anything to harm Silverlake again," he stammered.

"Mm-hmm, tell it to the judge." Deputy Amber stepped forward, placing Mayor Blackworth under arrest. The deputy didn't look me in the eye, and I was okay with that. I was just happy to see Amber wasn't blaming me for any part of this. She was probably still tired from her run in with the Sleep of the Dead.

Vance made his way through the crowd. "Can't leave you alone for two minutes, can I?"

"Not if you don't want to miss the action," I replied, brushing my hands together as if it had been easy peasy.

"What do you want to do now?" Vance asked.

I hadn't forgotten Vance's confession earlier that night. I still owed it to him to tell him how I felt. What he, no, what we chose to do with the knowledge was still up in the air. But I had to tell him tonight that I still cared for him before I chickened out. "There's actually something I want to talk to you about. Walk with me?" I motioned with my head to the path behind us. We could still nab the chocolates on the way.

Vance fell in step along side of me with Rocky right at his heels.

We walked forward for a moment, away from the gathering crowd and questions. I smiled and waved at Connie as we walked past the potion's shop. She was outside, closing up for the night, but she winked when she spotted me and Vance. I closed my eyes and gave a slight shake of my head, but a smiled tugged at the corner of my mouth.

The path was now mostly clear. Candles flicked inside jack-o-lanterns, and leaves rustled the trees. The air was still chilly, but not bitterly so, which was a relief seeing I no longer had my cloak.

I took a deep breath, feeling that it was now or never. What I hadn't anticipated was how nervous I'd be. My heart fluttered madly in my chest and my mouth went bone dry. I cleared my throat. "You said something tonight on the side of the road." I glanced up to read Vance's expression. He was still facing forward, walking in step with me, but he nodded. I took that as a sign to continue. "The thing is, you're right. I haven't been fair. I didn't want to see you dating someone else."

Vance stopped abruptly, and I did the same. It would have been easier to confess my thoughts to the cobblestone path or the nighttime sky, but I forced myself to meet Vance's eyes. What I saw there took my breath away. The full moon reflected off his light blue eyes, eyes filled with such hope, as they searched my face.

I took a fortifying breath, and then plowed forward. "I told you we were better off as friends because I was scared." I hadn't planned on saying that, but as I said the words, I knew they were true. "I've already told you how our breakup wrecked me, and I didn't want anyone to ever have that power over me again."

Vance began to speak, but I interrupted him by holding my hand up in a stopping motion.

"Let me finish." I closed my eyes and swallowed. "But I also realize that you can't love someone with reservations. That's not how love works. And I've also come to realize that no matter what the future holds, I'm a strong woman. A strong witch. I'll never run away again." Again, as I spoke the words, I knew they were true. I had learned more about myself in the last six months than in the previous decade. "Which leads me to say, I'm still stuck on you too." I gave Vance a weak smile and shrugged my shoulders. "I'm sorry I didn't say something sooner."

We had a moment where the two of us stared at one another, wondering what the other was thinking, wondering what our next steps were, wondering what either one of us wanted for the future when Vance reached out and cupped my cheek in the palm of his hand. He leaned down, and I met him halfway, closing the distance that separated us. Within a heartbeat, his lips were on mine, and the lock that had held my heart prisoner all those years, broke free.

"I've missed you," Vance murmured in the whisper of space that separated us.

"I've missed you, too."

Behind us, a chorus of hollers and whistles

erupted with Clemmie's cheers being the loudest "About time!" she called out.

I closed my eyes, and rested my forehead against Vance's, hoping everyone else would disappear. "So much for having a private moment."

"You know, I might know a spell."

"To make them disappear."

Vance nodded. It was a slight movement as we were still standing close together. I smiled at the thought.

Vance stepped back, his hand on my shoulders, so he could look at me. "You know I never meant to hurt you."

I swallowed. "I know." It was true. Vance wanted to explore the world, and I was ready to settle down right then and there. I could no longer fault him for following his heart and leaving. "We were young. We wanted different things."

"But not now."

I shook my head at a loss for words. Too overcome with emotions to speak.

Rocky barked and pranced around at our feet, apparently tired of all this lovey-dovey business.

I took Vance's hand and tugged him down the path, leaving the heavy emotions behind us and adding a layer of playfulness back to the evening. "What do you say we grab a couple of pumpkin spiced lattes with those chocolates and wrap this Halloween up right?"

"Lead the way." Vance's thumb rubbed the delicate skin on the top of my wrist as we walked. It was something he used to do years ago. I looked down at our intwined hands and smiled, hoping that next year's Halloween would have less hijinks but just as much magic.

ELEVEN

I woke up the next morning thinking about the previous day. What had started out as a crazy and chaotic Halloween had ended on a rather sweet note. One could say the holiday had encompassed both tricks and treats.

I got ready fairly quickly, which was surprising given last night had been such a late night when it was all said and done. Our group of friends had decided to meet up at Clemmie's this morning to help her put her shop back in order. No small feat, even with using magic. Last night, Aunt Thelma was overjoyed and relieved to have the antidote chocolate, but rather dismayed at seeing the box of kittens. My poor aunt had switched from croaking to sneezing in an instant. Who knew she was allergic to cats? It never seemed to bother her when I pranced around in my feline form, but then again, I was really a human underneath it all. Maybe that was the secret.

Thankfully, Margaret, our town healer's sister, had been able to take the kittens in the night before even though it had been close to eleven o'clock. I had forgotten Margaret ran a pet rescue. If I had remembered, I would've called her right off the bat.

When I went downstairs, Aunt Thelma had already left for the morning, which wasn't surprising. My aunt was much more of a morning person than I was, or should I say, had become since moving home. I found that I rather enjoyed sleeping in and staying up late versus surviving on caffeine and sugar, a habit I had developed in my former life running the rat race.

Coming down from the last step into the lobby, I spotted Percy behind the registration desk. Seeing the poltergeist reminded me of our talk last night. His head was resting on his fist, elbows bent on the countertop in front of him. A pile of spitballs sat abandoned next to him. Percy's expression looked forlorn and tugged at my heart. There was nothing sadder than a depressed poltergeist.

"Hey Percy, are you okay?"

Percy looked up at me briefly with his eyes only before casting his gaze back to the counter. He didn't utter a word.

I pressed on. "I'm sorry we didn't catch back up last night. After everything that happened, I honestly forgot." I stood still and waited for Percy to give me grief or guilt, something that would be within his normal mischievous character, but instead he just sighed.

"If you want, I'm free later this morning. We could go ask Mr. McCormick about the roses?"

"It's too late," Percy mumbled.

"What do you mean it's too late? I'm sure I can help you find all the right ingredients, and then you can perform your spell or whatever it is you're doing."

Percy pushed off from the counter. "You don't understand. It had to be done last night." He turned his back to me.

I furrowed my brow and thought. "Oh, because of the full moon?"

"No, because of Halloween."

"Ohhhhh." Percy caught my eye from over his shoulder. He looked dejected. I hated seeing him this way. "There has to be something we can do." I started to stay.

Percy cut me off. "There isn't. I guess I'll just have to try next year." With that statement, Percy sighed and then disappeared into thin air.

"Well, that's awful," I said to the empty lobby.

I waited for our Saturday morning help to arrive before slipping out the front door. Aunt Thelma, Percy, and I did a decent job of holding down the fort Monday through Friday, but ever since the fall festival, we'd had a steady stream of reservations, with weekends being the busiest. It was nice having the extra hands on deck to assist with check-ins and housekeeping.

"I have my cell phone on me. Call me if you need me," I told Emily on my way out the door.

Once outside, I debated my options. It was either take the long way on the main road around the lake or take the shortcut down the Enchanted Trail.

There was a time when I jogged the Enchanted Trail. As a child, I would escape to the trail every afternoon after school. Often pretending I was an explorer off in some exotic land, or the trail was the gateway to another realm or time. That was before I'd been attacked on the trail *and* found a dead body. Two separate incidences, months apart, mind you. Slowly, I had started taking the trail again, but rarely alone.

But something about my fresh start with Vance last night had me thinking that I wanted to make a fresh start in other areas of my life. If I was brave enough to tell Vance how I felt, then I was brave enough to walked down the Enchanted Trail alone. Well, with my wand out, that is. Didn't need to be reckless now, did I?

The morning air had a chill to it. It seemed the cold snap that had rolled through last night was sticking around. Clemmie wouldn't be happy; she hated the cold. I, on the other hand, was excited to pull out my hooded sweatshirts and thick, chunky sweaters. A girl down south didn't get much opportunity to wear her fall favorites. If I hadn't been on my way to clean up Sit For a Spell, I'd be wearing my chocolate leather boots, dark jeans, and orange knitted sweater. Come to think of it, that would be the perfect outfit to wear on a date with Vance, and I knew there would be a date in the near future. It was only a matter of when.

The leaves were still green and vibrant like the verdant grass, but I wasn't going to complain. While the leaves didn't change down here like they did in the Georgia mountains, they still did put on a show, especially the pecan trees with the elongated, jagged leaves turning a bright, lemony shade of yellow. That was still a few weeks off, which was okay. I was patient.

The walk down Enchanted Trail was surprisingly uneventful, or maybe that's the way that it was always supposed to be. Things in my life seemed to be clicking into place one by one. It felt good, really good. I always counted my blessings every night before bed, and lately the list had gotten quite long. I closed my eyes and took a deep breath as I walked, inhaling the fresh air and letting the sounds of nature wash over me. A witch could get used to this.

In front of me appeared the charming shops of Village Square. The peak of the bookstore's rusty red-clay roof, the highest rooftop in the shopping district, poked out from the treetops. In the distance, the clocktower chimed nine times, my footsteps walking in tempo with each note echoing across the lake. It was funny, during the hustle and bustle of the daytime, I never noticed the clocktower. But in the quiet moments such as this, it was impossible to ignore. The sound was quite soothing, reverent even. Like church bells on a Sunday morning.

The trail weaved the entire way around the lake and behind the back-facing shops, with several small footpaths worn into the dirt behind the individual stores. I veered off the Enchanted Trail coming up alongside the bookstore and cafe. I was tempted to stop in and pay Misty a visit and catch her up on everything that happened with Vance last night, but I didn't want to keep Clemmie waiting a moment longer. With that thought in mind, I picked up my pace and walked briskly to the tea shop. As the path swerved to the left, so did my head as I cocked it and tried to make out the scene before me.

"That's just wrong." Someone, probably a group of teenagers, had smashed the pumpkins in front of the stores. That wasn't all. The delinquents had shredded bales of hay and ripped the dried corn stalks from front porches, littering the remains amongst the fall gardens and trampling on mums in the process. In other words, they had destroyed the Village Square's Halloween decorations.

I thought back to my nighttime stroll with Vance. The shops had looked perfect then, meaning we couldn't blame the damage on Mayor Blackworth. I shook my head. The vandalism was more of a mess to clean up and really what no one needed at the moment, including Clemmie. Her shop hadn't been spared.

Oh no. My heart sank to my toes. I walked a few steps forward to Sit For a Spell's front porch. Clemmie had set out a beautiful Halloween-themed tea set on a black wrought iron table. The porcelain tea pot had been painted orange like a pumpkin with the lid painted soft green like a stem. Vines danced around the tea pot's middle. But now, the vandals had smashed the entire teapot on the porch. The remnants were strewn across the concrete. All that remained intact were the coordinating teacups.

I stepped forward to pick up the handle from the ground and spotted the largest piece of the pot behind the front azalea bush. I bent low to pick it up, and that's not all I spied. A scream threatened to rip out of my mouth as I came face-to-face with Mayor Blackworth's dead body. I jumped back, stumbling over my feet as I scurried back to the footpath.

Diane chose that moment to arrive.

"Hello! I brought the coffee!" Diane held up the cardboard carrier balanced evenly with four to-go cups on each side.

I put out my hand in a warning motion. "Stay there." I couldn't say anything else. My mind was reeling. My heart was racing. And I wanted to save Diane from the ghastly sight.

"What's wrong?" Diane, who had been walking briskly down the path came to a screeching halt.

I stared at her for a moment until I found my voice. "It's Mayor Blackworth. He's dead."

"What? Are you sure?"

I blinked back at Diane.

"Scratch that, of course, you're sure. What do we do?"

"We need to call it in. Where's Clemmie?" I looked through the display window of Clemmie's shop and was surprised to find that she wasn't inside yet. I thought for sure she would have beat us here this morning. Clemmie was never one to wait around for help to arrive.

"Here," Diane held the cardboard carrier out for me to take the coffee from her. I walked over and did just that. "I'll call the sheriff's department."

I nodded my thanks. While we stood there and Diane made the call, I started to take in the scene around me. I had already noticed the destroyed decorations and the teapot. A realization hit me. What if the teapot was the murder weapon? I gulped and wiped my hand nervously off on my leggings. It was too late now. My fingerprints were already all over the piece, along with dozens of others who had probably picked up the teapot to admire it. Behind me,

Diane relayed the details of our location and discovery.

"He's definitely dead," I heard her say. Diane's words continued buzzing in the background as I inched closer to Mayor Blackworth's body, wondering if the cause of death was apparent. The phone conversation now sounded so far away.

Stealing my resolve, I took a steadying breath and crouched low to the ground. Mayor Blackworth was lying toes up, his head turned to the side. Blood pooled beneath it. I sucked in a breath and eyed the remnants of the teapot shattered on the porch. I stood up and scanned the body from a different angle, and that was when my heart clenched in my chest. I hadn't noticed it at first, but now there was no denying it. Mayor Blackworth had been eating one of the candied apples from The Candy Cauldron when he died. The half-eaten apple lay on the ground beside him. The stick was still clutched in his black-ened fist. I knew enough about magic to know the discoloration of Blackworth's hand was the result of a curse. A powerful curse if it was able to turn his hand black.

"Oh no. No, it can't be the apple."

"What's that?" Diane had ended the phone call and was keeping her distance, but yet she had still picked up on what I had said. I looked back at her, unsure what to say. I was scared to share my suspicion concerning the candied apple. Could the treat have somehow been at fault? I couldn't help but think of Beatrice and Sabrina and the prank they had played last night. I prayed that they hadn't messed with the apples, but I honestly wouldn't have put it past them. A thought that made me feel sick to my stomach. Not to mention the fact that I had given Mayor Blackworth the apples. Of course, he was supposed deliver them to Misty, but still, I might have had a role to play in this as well.

All these thoughts and more raced through my mind in the seconds after Diane's question.

"What are y'all up to?" Clemmie walked up and joined us. Her eyes looked at Diane and back to me, waiting for one of us to answer. Her expression looked impatient.

"Um," I cleared my throat and looked at Diane.

Diane blinked in rapid succession. "You see. It's just that," she looked back over to me.

"Er..."

"Well, spit it out." Clemmie placed her fisted hand on her hip.

I furrowed my brow, found my voice, and said, "Mayor Blackworth is dead. His body is right here." I pointed to where Blackworth's body rested between the azalea bushes and porch. I looked over at the body again and thought the man might have even hit his head on the brick landscaping border as he went down.

"Say what?" Clemmie replied, even though she

heard us perfectly well. She rolled up on the balls of her feet to take a look, but stayed rooted to the spot. "I would say who would do such a thing, but we all know perfectly well that the list is long."

Diane nodded solemnly. "I already called the sheriff's department. Someone should be here in a minute."

"Well, nothing we can do but wait until they arrive."

No sooner had Clemmie pronounced the obvious than Deputy Jones arrived on the scene. I had to admit that I was mighty happy to see Deputy Jones and not his partner. Although perhaps I should wait to count my blessings. Amber could be right behind him. I peered hopefully over his shoulder to see who else was coming down the path and was relieved when I saw that it was Dr. Fitz, the town medical examiner. Dr. Fitz made the perfect medical examiner. Even in his advancing years, he was unnaturally strong thanks to his werewolf genes, and his animal instincts were always on point. Even now as he examined the scene, his nose was twitching, and his bushy eyebrows were pulled down in concentration. It was almost as if he was picking up another animal scent. Diane, Clemmie, and I watched with morbid curiosity.

Dr. Fitz seemed on to something. He circled around the body, as close as he could with the bushes and porch in his way, walking around the bushes and standing on the porch as needed. He then bent low to the body and cautiously sniffed. Dr. Fitz instantly pulled back and brushed his nose with the back of his hand, shaking his head in the process.

"He didn't like that," Clemmie muttered.

"Wonder what he smelled," Diane asked under her breath.

"Nothing good," I added.

"Ms. Nightingale?" I snapped my head up. Deputy Jones interrupted our side conversation and called me forward. "I understand you found the body?"

"Unfortunately. I was on my way to meet up with these ladies and clean up Clemmie's shop." I pointed Diane and Clemmie in turn.

"What's wrong with your shop?" Deputy Jones asked Clemmie before turning and looking in the front window. His eyes widened in surprise. The destruction inside was apparent twenty feet away.

"Blackworth unleashed a flock of pixies, that's what," Clemmie said in a huff.

"As in Mayor Blackworth?" Deputy Jones motioned to the body with his ink pen in hand.

"The one and only as far as I know." Clemmie scowled at the dead man. Even in death, he couldn't be restored to her good graces.

"I hadn't heard," Deputy Jones said by way of explanation.

"Sounds like Mayor Blackworth made quite a mess for himself last night." Dr. Fitz joined us.

"Speaking of which, how did Mayor Blackworth end up here last night anyway? Last I saw him, Amber was placing him under arrest," I said.

"They let him go," Deputy Jones said matter of factly.

"What?!" Our trio replied in chorus.

"The sheriff and the DA decided not to press charges," Deputy Jones shrugged his shoulders as if to say that was the end of it.

"Sounds like some dirty politics going on right there," Clemmie grumbled.

I had to agree with her. Surely there was enough evidence to prosecute the former mayor. It was a moot point now, but still worth looking into in my opinion.

"Deputy, a word." Dr. Fitz motioned for Deputy Jones to join him out of earshot.

The deputy turned to us. "Ladies, you're free to go. I'll be in touch if I have any questions." He nodded his dismissal, and our trio turned to walk around the back of the shop, but my conscious got the best of me.

"I'm going to run a quick errand. I'll be right back," I said to Diane and Clemmie, and jogged off before they could ask any questions.

It wasn't a lie. I really did have an errand to run. I wanted to give Luke a heads up about the candied apple. I didn't know if the confection would come into play, but I still wanted Luke to know that the sheriff might come calling.

On my quick walk to The Candy Cauldron, I pulled out my phone and dialed Vance.

"Are you okay?" Vance asked when our lines connected.

"You already heard?"

"I'm down at the station. The Robertson boys were arrested for vandalism last night, and their parents asked me to represent them when your call came in."

"Did they hit up the Village Square?"

"Not that I know of." Vance sounded unsure.

"Well, someone did. It's a mess here."

"I'll find out. But what about you?"

"I'm okay, just a little shaky." I hadn't realized just how much stumbling on Blackworth's body had upset me until that moment. The adrenaline was starting to wear off, and reality was starting to set in, along with my determination. I knew I wouldn't feel settled until the case was solved.

"I should be done within the hour, and I can meet up with you."

"Thanks, I'm headed to The Candy Cauldron right now. I'll explain in a little bit. Meet me at Sit For a Spell? I still need to help Clemmie clean up."

"I'll see you there."

I hung up with Vance and strolled into the candy shop.

"Hello?" I called out into the empty store. If Halloween was the busiest day of the year, then I had a feeling the day after Halloween was the slowest. I couldn't imagine any parent taking their child to a candy store on November first. Kids were probably still on a sugar high from the night before.

"Luke?" I called out again. "Are you here?"

Luke poked his head out from the kitchen.

"Hey Angelica, what's going on?"

"Hey, there's something I need to tell you."

"Is everything okay?" Luke walked fully out from the back and met me at the counter.

"I'm not sure." I decided to cut right to the chase. "I just found Mayor Blackworth's body. He died outside of the tea shop."

"What? That's awful," Luke instantly replied.

"It is." I paused for a moment.

"What aren't you telling me?"

"It might be nothing, but he had one of your candied apples in his hand, and it was black."

"The apple?"

I gulped. "No, his hand."

Luke paled. "He didn't buy it from me." He shook his head in denial.

"No, he got it from me."

"How?"

"I ran into him on my way back to the bookstore

with Misty's order. I asked him to deliver them for me before I even knew who he was."

"Only he never did."

"Exactly. It might be nothing, but I just wanted to let you know." The implication hung in the air.

"The twins wouldn't have done anything like that on purpose." Luke said in hushed tones.

"No, they wouldn't." Sabrina and Beatrice liked to play tricks, but they wouldn't hurt anyone intentionally. Unfortunately, sometimes our actions have unforeseen outcomes, like last night's frog curse.

Luke must've been thinking the same thing as me. "I need to call my sister."

"I thought you might. I'll be down at Clemmie's. If you hear anything, or need to talk, give my cell a call." I turned to walk away and had the door pushed halfway open when Luke called from behind me.

"Hey Angelica? Thanks for letting me know."

I nodded. "Of course."

TWELVE

The cleaning was well underway by the time I got back to Sit For a Spell. Clemmie and Diane had been joined by Diane's boyfriend, Roger, and Aunt Thelma. The four of them had made a big dent in the mess.

Roger lined up black trash bags full of debris along the front inside window while Diane righted the tables and chairs. Aunt Thelma trailed after her, wiping the tabletops down with a soapy cloth. Clemmie worked on salvaging whatever stock she could, rearranging the shelves to make them look as full as possible.

"I am just going to have to file an insurance claim. That's all there is to it," Clemmie remarked while eyeing her now mostly empty shelves. The pixies had destroyed more than they had left intact. Only a handful of mugs remained, and almost every teapot was either chipped, cracked, or smashed completely. Not to mention all the loose-leaf tea that had been dumped onto the floor and thrown about. That took forever to pick up. The tea was stuck in every nook and cranny. I was convinced Clemmie would find loose tea for months to come.

It took over an hour, but at last we were finished picking up the store.

"At least those rotten pixies didn't get my holiday stock. The storage room is locked up tight." Clemmie walked out from the back and joined us. With the cleaning done, we all took a seat at the round tables where patrons usually relaxed with their afternoon tea.

"I'd say that Mayor Blackworth needs to pay for what he's done, but he surely already has," Roger remarked.

Vance appeared outside the door at that moment. Clemmie stood up and trotted over to unlock the deadbolt for him to come in.

"Hey guys, sorry I couldn't get here any sooner."

We all spoke up at the same time, talking over one another and telling Vance that it was okay. Roger offered Vance a seat, which he readily accepted.

Diane brought the conversation back to the murder. "Who do you guys think did it?"

"How did they do it? Do you think he was cursed?" Aunt Thelma fidgeted with the gold necklace around her neck.

"I'm not sure. It looked like he was bleeding from the back of his head." I then debated telling the group about the apple but decided there was no point keeping it a secret. They would find out about it sooner or later and maybe they might have another explanation for it all. "He also was eating one of Luke's candied apples, and his hand was black."

A collective gasp filled the air.

"You don't think those girls cursed the apples, do you?" Aunt Thelma asked. Her hand moved from her necklace to her throat, no doubt remembering what it felt like to croak.

"They do like to make trouble," Clemmie quipped.

"Trouble, maybe, but those girls wouldn't put a death curse on anyone," Diane said.

"Not on purpose," Roger added.

"Which is exactly what Luke and I thought. He's calling Sally and talking to the girls." The group was silent as we individually were lost in our thoughts. "I also saw that your pumpkin teapot was smashed out front," I started to say.

"Do you think it's the murder weapon?" Aunt Thelma asked.

"I'm not sure. I mean, it could be," I said.

"Or it could have been the Robertson kids. They've got a couple charges against them for vandalism already." Vance filled our group in on Terry and Tommy Reynolds being arrested the night before and their parents hiring Vance to represent them. The Reynolds were a rather wealthy family living in an old Victorian by the business district. Mrs. Reynolds knew her boys were troublemakers, but good luck getting her to admit to it in public. No, in public they were her perfect little angels. It was embarrassing how much their parents tried to cover up their misdeeds. Last month it was spray painting the high school gym. Who knew what they'd do next?

"Both troublemakers, that's what they are. Find out if they smashed my teapot, will you?" Clemmie asked Vance.

Vance nodded that he would.

"What about suspects?" Diane asked the group.

"Who isn't one?" I asked.

"That's a good point. I heard Pete Sutherland got into it with Blackworth as Amber was arresting him," Roger said. Pete Sutherland was the high school baseball coach and science teacher, in that order.

"What was his problem?" Diane asked.

"Pete was stuck in the maze asleep with his two kids most the evening."

"I don't blame him one bit then," Clemmie remarked.

"Quite a few people were stuck in there." I thought back to the line of people the fire department had rescued.

"This is just awful," Aunt Thelma said.

We all agreed that it was.

"And then you had those creepy decorations."
Diane held her hands back in fright.

"What creepy decorations?" Aunt Thelma asked.
I forgot that she had spent most of the night tucked
safely away at the inn.

"Blackworth bewitched skeletons, scarecrows,
spiders, you name it, to come to life and scare
people," Vance explained.

"Rotten man. Sorry, and I know it's not polite to
speak ill of the dead," Diane said thinking better of it.
Roger rubbed her back in a comforting gesture.

"No, it was pretty rotten of him," Vance agreed.

"Well, you know you have to add my name to the
list. The police are going to." No one wanted to agree
with Clemmie, but she was right. Mayor Blackworth
had destroyed her store and was found dead out in
front of it. If I didn't know Clemmie, I'd consider her
a suspect too.

"I'm keeping you on retainer," Clemmie pointed
at Vance.

"Yes ma'am," Vance replied.

"Well, if they're going to investigate you, then
they have to look at Mayor Parrish as well," Diane
said thoughtfully.

"What's Mayor Parrish have to do with all this?"
Aunt Thelma asked.

"She was hotter than a jerry-rigged witch at a pie

eatin' contest trying to ruin Silverlake's Halloween," Clemmie explained.

"Now there's a motive," Roger added.

"Wonder if she has an alibi." Vance thought aloud.

"I think we should be writing this down." Diane stood and walked over to her purse presumably to retrieve a pen and paper.

"I'd offer you paper, but those darn pixies shredded it all." Clemmie was still visibly annoyed at the miniature troublemakers.

"What about Mr. McCormick?" Vance pondered.

"He was pretty worried about his daughter." I picked up Vance's trail of thought.

"Downright distraught, I heard," Clemmie nodded in agreement.

"Mike wouldn't do any such thing. He doesn't have a mean bone in his body." I had to agree with Aunt Thelma. Mr. McCormick wasn't the type of man to seek revenge. Then again, all bets were off when it came to family. People had a tendency to act in all sorts of ways out of character when it came to defending their family members.

I shared my thoughts with the group.

"I agree. It's not like Mr. McCormick to react in anger, but who's to say that a simple altercation didn't get out of hand?" Diane shook her head as she scribbled notes down on a scrap piece of paper.

"With the teapot right in arms reach," Clemmie gripped for an invisible tea pot.

"Now this is just ridiculous. Mike McCormick didn't kill Mayor Blackworth." Aunt Thelma placed her hands on her hips as she spoke her mind, daring any of us to contradict her.

"Well, someone sure did," Clemmie quipped.

"I say we keep our nose down and leave this one to the police," Aunt Thelma declared.

"Easy for you to say. You're not a suspect." Clemmie crossed her hands in front of her chest.

"You're not either. Not yet anyway. And maybe not ever. I think we've gotten ahead of ourselves, here. I also say this meeting is officially adjourned. I'm sure you all have better things to do with your Saturday morning."

I looked over to Vance at the same time that Diane locked eyes with Roger.

"Not really," Roger said summing up all of our feelings.

"Well, I do. So, if you don't mind, I'll catch up with you folks later. Oh! That reminds me. I'm hosting a dinner tonight, and you're all invited. Something to take our minds off this ghastly murder business and help us enjoy fall. It is my favorite season after all, and Thanksgiving seems so far away. I'll see you all at the inn, say six o'clock?"

Everyone agreed that that would work.

"What would you like me to bring?" Diane asked Aunt Thelma.

The two ladies continued their discussion over the menu while I turned my attention to Vance.

"You sure you're okay?" Vance assessed me with his eyes.

"Feeling better by the minute actually."

"You're not going to drop this are you?"

I knew what Vance meant. "No, do you want me to?"

"No. I didn't know Blackworth, but I know Sheriff Reynolds, and unfortunately Clemmie is right."

"They'll set their eyes on her or someone else equally innocent."

"Exactly. Listen, I have to go and let Rocky out. Who knows what he's done to my place since this morning. Then I have to get back to work, but I'll see you tonight?"

"Sounds good." I turned around and noticed everyone staring at us.

Aunt Thelma clapped her hands together. "I'm so glad you two are back together."

"Took you long enough," Clemmie said with a wink.

"If you want a wedding cake, you know who to come see," Diane smiled.

"And flowers," Roger chuckled, raising one finger in the air.

Both Vance and I stammered our excuses, talking over one another. We were not there yet. We were taking things slow, if that was even possible given our history. The sight of our unease only made our friends laugh and tease even more.

"You guys are awful," I said even though I too was smiling.

Vance gave my hand a squeeze and left a moment later.

"Aunt Thelma, can I talk to you for a moment?" I pulled my aunt off to the side.

"What is it, dear? You know we were only joking."

"Oh yeah, no. This isn't anything about that. I want to talk to you about Percy. Something's going on with him. He was trying to get the ingredients for a spell last night, and I guess it could only be performed on Halloween. When I saw him this morning, he was so down, it's not like him. Not like him at all." Percy was always playing practical jokes like putting salt in my coffee or unscrewing the ketchup lid so when I went to squeeze a dollop on a hamburger a massive glop fell out, drowning my supper. This somber version of the elderly poltergeist did not jive with the ghost I knew at all.

"I don't know anything about a spell, but I do know that he's sweet on Eleanor. You know, the ghost that haunts the tavern, but that's all I know."

"I thought Melanie the banshee haunted the tavern."

"Not exclusively. As far as I know, Eleanor never leaves the place. She's related to Bonnie somehow, I believe. Not exactly sure of the relationship." Bonnie and her husband Craig co-owned the tavern. I liked Bonnie, or as Craig liked to refer to her, his better half.

Something told me that if I wanted to get to the bottom of Percy's odd behavior, I'd have to pay a visit to Eleanor, which was exactly what I was going to do.

THIRTEEN

With my mind made up, I headed to the tavern. The establishment was technically called Dragon's Mead, but all the locals referred to it as the tavern.

In a way, I was honoring Aunt Thelma's request and not investigating the murder, if only for an hour or two.

"Hi Bonnie," I said as I sidled up to the bar. The lunch crowd had settled in for their afternoon burgers and beer, and I was tempted to do the same, but first I wanted to talk to Eleanor if that was at all possible.

"Well, if it isn't the talk of the town." Bonnie said as she wiped the mahogany bar top down in front of me.

"I don't know about that." Bonnie's comment caught me off guard.

"Heard you found Blackworth," she said glancing up, while continuing to clean.

"Oh, that."

"What did you think I was talking about? You and that handsome boyfriend of yours?" Bonnie let out a bark of laughter. The sound was rich and throaty and made me smile. Bonnie's laugh was the type of laughter you could hear clear across the bar, and you always wanted to know what was so funny.

I felt my cheeks turn pink despite my best efforts not to blush. I only had myself to blame for kissing Vance in such a public manner. Something that I couldn't bring myself to regret, not even a little bit. Because part of me agreed with everyone else. It was about time for me and Vance to get back together.

"What can I get for you?" Bonnie looked at me expectantly.

"Actually, I was wondering if I could talk to Eleanor if she was in."

Bonnie gave me a queer look.

Right, Eleanor never left.

I quickly revised my statement. "Or if you could just tell her I was looking for her? Truthfully, Percy has been acting a little off, and I was hoping Eleanor could clue me in as to why. Aunt Thelma said that he's been spending a bit of time with her."

"That he has. Hold on just a moment." Bonnie disappeared in the back, and I waited patiently for her to come back.

As I waited, I people-watched. I had to admit I was pleasantly surprised with how busy the tavern was. The fall festival looked to have drummed up business for everyone. That was the purpose of it, after all.

"Angelica, meet my great, great Aunt Eleanor." A sweet older, slightly transparent lady appeared behind Bonnie.

"How do you do, Miss?" she said by way of greeting.

"Nice to meet you. I was wondering if you had a moment to chat?"

"Time is all I have," the kind ghost said with a sad smile.

"I'll just leave you to your chat. Another beer, Carl?" Bonnie hollered down to a gentleman at the end of the bar.

The older lady motioned for me to join her in the corner booth. I stood from the barstool and followed, noticing how the ghost moved around the furniture and people as if she were still alive, unlike the other ghosts I knew. Percy tended to walk right through things or disappear and pop up into place without notice.

We got settled across from one another.

"Bonnie said you wanted to talk to me about Percy?"

"Yes. The thing is, he's been acting troubled

lately, and I'm worried about him. I was hoping you could help me figure out why."

"Percy really is a sweet man." If a ghost could blush, Eleanor would. I was sure of it. I quickly realized that the admiration went both ways.

I skipped the pleasantries. "Is everything okay?" I leaned forward as if speaking in confidence.

"I don't know how much you know about me and my past."

"Nothing at all."

"I see." Eleanor closed her eyes and nodded her head as if making up her mind. When she opened them again, her expression looked pained as she said, "I'm trapped here."

"I beg your pardon?" I couldn't have heard her right.

"I have been, for over two hundred years."

"You're trapped? You mean like here on Earth." I knew there were some ghosts who couldn't cross over, or didn't want to, but I didn't know the details. Take Percy, for example. As far as I knew, he was free to head on up to heaven any time he felt like it, except he liked it here, tormenting the living as he once put it.

"No, I mean here at the tavern. I haven't stepped foot outside of the property since eighteen fourteen."

My mouth dropped open slightly. "Oh my gosh."

"It's a curse. And there's nothing I or my family have ever been able to do to break it."

"But Percy is trying to."

Eleanor nodded her head. "Like I said, he's a very sweet man. Once he heard my story, he vowed he would do everything he could to break it."

"Which explains why he's leaving the inn more and more."

"It seems that once your aunt started to put a little faith in him, he rose to the occasion. Or so that's the way he tells it. He's becoming more and more the man he used to be and less of a trickster." But even as Eleanor said the word, a sparkle returned to her eye. She seemed to like Percy's mischievous ways.

"How did it happen? I'm sorry, if that's too personal, forget I asked."

"You mean the curse?"

I nodded.

"Foolishness. On my part and Oscar's."

"Who's Oscar?"

"He was my fiancé and didn't take too kindly to me leaving him at the altar. But he wasn't nearly as upset as his mother was. Tabatha was a powerful witch, not to be messed with. A lesson I found out the hard way."

"She cursed you for leaving her son."

"She did. The match was all wrong. We would've been miserable together. Oscar agreed with me after the fact. Oh, he hated me for a while there. But saw the reason when he finally met his true love. By then, the damage was done. His mother said that I might find love during my lifetime, but I would spend an eternity alone. At the time, I didn't understand what she meant, but on the day I died, it all became crystal clear."

"The tavern?"

"Was my family home. I've lived in the apartment upstairs ever since."

"And you're all alone?"

"Well, not exactly. My sister pops in from time to time. She haunts a lovely cottage in Surrey. Of course, she's free to come and go as she pleases. I've always wanted to visit her though. Don't get me wrong, I've loved seeing my family grow through the years, but my loved ones come and go and yet here I still remain."

"I'm so sorry." I reached my hand across the table to offer the kind ghost comfort. Eleanor placed her hand within mine. Coolness washed over me from her after-life touch. I understood Percy's anguish for wanting to help and not being able to do anything.

Neither one of us said anything for a moment.

Bonnie made an appearance and broke the silence.

"I see you heard our family's sad tale." Bonnie placed an ice-cold Coke in front of me.

"It's awful. I'm so sorry." This time my apology was directed towards Bonnie.

"We've tried everything over the years. Even had a direct descendent of Oscar's give us a bit of blood. For a potion," Bonnie quickly supplied at my confused expression.

"But yet, here I still am." Eleanor seemed resigned to her fate.

"There has to be something we can do."

"I have no doubt that if anyone can solve this mystery, it's you Angelica." Bonnie patted the table before turning to see to her other customers.

"I'll try." I met Eleanor's gaze. Her expression looked forlorn, and for some reason, that only made me want to try all the more.

Later that night at dinner, I brought up Eleanor's curse. "I have another mystery I could use everyone's help with."

We were all seated around Aunt Thelma's dining room table upstairs in her third-floor apartment. Aunt Thelma may have agreed to let me bring the rest of the inn into the twenty-first century, but her private apartments were still very much stuck in the nineteen hundreds. Nineteen sixty to be exact. Aunt Thelma's apartment fully embodied the woman, right down to the pink shag carpet and gold decor. The style, like my aunt's strawberry-blonde locks, hadn't changed since I was a little girl, and somehow it was finding itself back in style.

I took a few minutes to reiterate my afternoon visit to the tavern and meeting with Eleanor.

"I didn't realize she couldn't leave," Diane said while scooping sweet potato casserole onto her plate.

"Bonnie doesn't like to talk about it." Aunt Thelma passed the green bean casserole to Roger.

"It's not her fault her great, great aunt was cursed. It's a black mark on that Oscar fellow's family. Shame on them for not breaking it." Clemmie didn't even look up from buttering her cornbread.

"Bonnie did say Oscar's descendants have been helpful, or maybe that's not the right word. From my understanding, they're not actively trying to break the curse, but they're willing to assist when asked."

"If they were so helpful, you'd think the curse would be broken," Roger mumbled in between scoops of cranberry dressing.

"Has anyone thought about reaching out to Tabitha?" Vance asked me directly.

"Not that I know of. But Eleanor said she was quite the nasty witch. I'm not sure if she'll be helpful or not."

"Two hundred years is a long time to hold a grudge. Maybe her ghost would be receptive," Diane offered helpfully.

"Or her spirit's as nasty as ever and she'll curse you too," Clemmie said.

"I forbid you from reaching out to her. It's too dangerous." Aunt Thelma's expression was fraught with worry.

"Now you've done it. The surefire way to get

Angelica to do something is to forbid her to do it." Roger jested.

"Angelica, don't listen to Roger. I want to help Eleanor too, but there has to be another way. I've heard stories about Tabitha. She was an evil woman. Her ghost won't be kind. She won't suddenly have a conscience."

"For all I know, Bonnie has already reached out to her. And trust me, I'm not looking to be cursed." My life was finally where I wanted it to be. I wasn't going to go muck it up now. "I have no intention of reaching out to Tabitha."

"It does make me wonder. What gives a curse power? Would it have been broken when Tabitha died?" Most of the curses that I knew of were bound by life-and-death, but I admit that I wasn't an expert.

"That's an interesting question." Roger cocked his head to the side. "I don't think I've ever thought about it before."

"It makes you wonder what Tabitha cursed." Diane stared unfocused at her plate.

"Because if it was Eleanor, the curse would've been broken when she died," Vance surmised.

"Right, it's what makes me think that Tabitha cursed something else. Maybe something in Eleanor's possession or the tavern itself?" Diane asked.

"Tabitha was something else. She gave us all a bad name. No wonder they wanted to burn our lot at the stake. I can't stand witches like that," Clemmie bristled.

Everyone's plates sat untouched.

I thought about Diane's question. "You know, I talked to Connie yesterday about curses when Aunt Thelma was croaking. She said that they can be tricky and asked if Aunt Thelma had recently bought any jewelry."

"You think Tabitha cursed a family heirloom?" Clemmie asked.

"I'm thinking it's possible. It would make sense that it's something that's been passed down from generation to generation to still keep the curse in effect," I said.

"But is it something on Eleanor's side of the family or Tabitha's?" Vance wondered.

My stomach sank to my toes. If it was an heirloom on Eleanor's side of the family, it should be pretty easy to figure out. If it was on Oscar's side of the family, that was another matter entirely. I didn't even know Oscar's surname.

"And what if somebody sold the heirloom? How are we ever going to find it?" Aunt Thelma asked.

"That would pose another problem," Roger stated the obvious.

"Needle in a haystack, that's what it would be," Clemmie remarked.

"It's a start, though." Vance looked over to me.

"You're right. I can ask Bonnie or Eleanor about it tomorrow."

"Good, now that that is settled, let's eat." Aunt Thelma's declaration put an end to the topic of conversation, and we all knew better than to bring it up again. Not if my aunt wanted to enjoy her meal. After missing Halloween last night, I'd hate to ruin dinner.

FOURTEEN

The next day was Sunday and my favorite day of the week. If Saturday was for running errands and catching up with friends, then Sunday was for catching up on sleep. Which was why, I fully intended on ignoring my cell phone when it started ringing on my bedside table. I managed to ignore it the first time, barely even cracking open an eye, but when my text messages started chiming and the phone continued ringing, I knew something important was happening

"Hello?" My voice was thick with sleep. I hadn't recognized the number when I answered.

"Where's Vance?" Clemmie asked without preamble.

"What?" I sat up in bed and cleared my throat. Clearly, I was missing some important pieces of the conversation.

"I need to find your boyfriend. Sheriff Reynolds brought me in for questioning. They ransacked my shop and my home this morning. They won't even tell me what they found."

"Hang on, the sheriff searched your house this morning?"

"And my shop. Keep up with me. I told the sheriff I won't talk to him without my lawyer present. Do you know where Vance is?"

"Er, I have no idea." I looked over at my alarm clock. It was almost nine o'clock, not as early as I initially thought.

"What do you mean you have no idea? Isn't he your boyfriend?"

"That doesn't mean I know where he is at all times." Clemmie was being a bit ridiculous, but I wasn't about to tell her that. I understood she was under a lot of stress, and frankly, she sounded panicked. "But don't worry, we'll find him. I'll keep trying to call his phone, and I'll head down to the station. He might already be there." If he wasn't in his home or office, Vance was usually at the sheriff's department or city hall. Seeing it was Sunday, city hall was closed, so he was most likely already at the sheriff's department. I wouldn't put it past Sheriff Reynolds or his daughter to withhold that information from Clemmie. It was just a type of tactic the sheriff would use to get Clemmie to agree to an interview without Vance present.

When I got downstairs, Percy was nowhere to be found. In fact, I hadn't seen the poltergeist since the previous morning. I wanted to tell him that I had spoken to Eleanor and wanted to help. Hopefully, he would turn up sooner rather than later and we could work together to help the sweet ghost out. I shook my head. Who would've thought the day would come when Percy and I would work together to solve a mystery? I suppose stranger things have happened, although at that moment, I couldn't think of one.

Aunt Thelma stood at Percy's post behind the registration desk.

"Everything okay, dear? You're up and about awfully early for a Sunday."

"Clemmie woke me up. She's been taken in for questioning, and she can't get hold of Vance."

"My word, that is troubling." Concern flooded my aunt's eyes. "I hate to say that she called it." Aunt Thelma couldn't hide the disappointment in her voice.

"I know. She said they searched her home and the shop this morning too."

"Oh, my."

"I told her I'd try and track down Vance."

"He's probably already there."

"That's what I'm hoping." In the ten minutes since I'd gotten off the phone with Clemmie, I mentally put together a list of where else Vance could be. I supposed he could also be grocery shopping or out for a run. The Enchanted Trail didn't make him jittery like me, and that's probably where he was.

I sighed.

Aunt Thelma looked at me expectantly.

"I really don't want to go for a run."

That got a chuckle out of my aunt. "You are my niece, aren't you."

I smiled warmly in response. And then my expression turned somber. Did I check the trail or the sheriff's department first? Which was quicker? "I guess I'm headed to see Sheriff Reynolds. Cross your fingers for me."

"Here, take my car. I don't have any place to be until later this afternoon." Aunt Thelma pulled her car keys out from under the counter and held them out for me.

"Thanks." I readily took the keys and pocketed them. I had been debating for months about getting my own car, but Aunt Thelma insisted she didn't mind sharing, and I was slowly coming around to agreeing with her. Plus, I really didn't want a car payment.

When I pulled into the sheriff's department lot, I noticed Mrs. Potts pacing out front. She was dressed in her Sunday best, wearing a cornflower blue dress and coordinating bonnet and purse. The poor woman kept fidgeting with her purse strap and glancing up at the sheriff's department front door.

"That's odd." I shifted the car into park and got out.

Mrs. Potts was mumbling to herself. She seemed so out of sorts that I wondered if she had been spelled, perhaps a curse left over from Halloween night. I had seen firsthand what a berdévo spell could do, making people act a bit nutty, and that's exactly what Mrs. Potts looked like.

"Mrs. Potts, are you okay?"

The older lady visibly startled.

"Sorry, I didn't mean to scare you."

"No, that's quite alright. I'm afraid I'm lost in my own thoughts. Just having a little talk with myself." Mrs. Potts' clear blue eyes locked with mine, and I could tell she was as sane as ever.

"Is there something I can do?"

"Well, I'm afraid I'm in a bit of a pickle. I saw something night before last, and I'm trying to decide if it's worth telling the sheriff or not. I don't want to cause any trouble." Mrs. Potts' eyes darted from side to side as she stood on the bottom step before looking over her shoulder once more at the front door.

I searched my old second-grade teacher's expression. The poor woman was downright distraught. I carefully thought out my words as I spoke. "If it relates to a crime, you should probably tell the sheriff."

"I'm not sure if it does, to tell you the truth."

"Do you want to tell me about it and maybe I can help?"

Mrs. Potts hesitated. "I suppose I could do that." she said after a moment. I waited for Mrs. Potts to continue. She looked back at the building one more time before saying, "I saw Chief Grady arguing with that Mr. Blackworth fellow Halloween night."

My eyebrows shot up. I fought the urge to not interrupt.

"I was walking Mitzie, you know, my maltese when I stumbled upon the two men."

This time I couldn't help but ask, "What time was this?"

"Oh, I'd say a little after eleven. I don't normally walk Mitzie that late, but she was so nerved up from all the trick-or-treaters. The poor girl couldn't settle down, and I knew neither one of us would get any sleep until she did."

I nodded encouragingly for Mrs. Potts to continue.

"Anyhow, that Mr. Blackworth was taking pictures outside of Clemmie's shop. He seemed pretty proud of his handiwork if his smile was any indication." Mrs. Potts looked up at me and arched her eyebrows, telling me exactly what she thought about that.

My expression mirrored her own, first because Blackworth had been pleased at the destruction, and second because the location was where I had found his body.

"I know. He was positively beaming as he took it all in."

"That's horrible."

"Oh, believe me, I agree with you. So did Chief Grady. He told Blackworth that he had no business still being in town. Then, when Blackworth replied something cheeky, I thought Chief Grady was going to deck him. Mind you, not that he didn't deserve it. Chief Grady told Blackworth that he had hurt a lot of people that night."

"But he didn't hit him." It was a statement, not a question.

"No, Blackworth was alive and well when the chief walked away. He didn't hurt him."

"Well, that's good." I was hoping that the fire chief was innocent even if the time and place were highly suspect.

"It's just that—" Mrs. Potts began fidgeting with the strap of her purse.

"Excuse me, did you say Blackworth as in Mayor Blackworth?" Mrs. Potts and I turned to look at the woman who had joined us. She had short red hair and freckles, and I'd say she was somewhere in her mid-thirties. She wasn't a local, but she wasn't glowing either, which meant she was a supernatural of some sort.

"Yes, that's right." Mrs. Potts hesitated before answering, her voice wobbling a bit.

"Oh no, how bad is it?" The woman asked.

"What do you mean?" I cocked my head to the side.

"How much trouble is he in?" The woman put her hands on her hips and stared over my shoulder at the sheriff's department. "I told him not to do it, but does he ever listen to me? No. Thinks I'll just clean up his messes every time."

Mrs. Potts blinked at the woman as if trying to make sense of who she was and where she had come from.

"I'm sorry, have we met?" I asked.

"I'm sorry, where are my manners? I'm Elizabeth Webb, Mayor Blackworth's assistant, of sorts." Elizabeth held out her hand, and I shook it, followed by Mrs. Potts. "Has he been arrested then? I figured that's what happened when I didn't hear from him yesterday."

I looked to Mrs. Potts, but she wouldn't meet my eyes. No way was my former teacher about to break the news to this woman. I cleared my throat. "I hate to be the one to tell you and have you find out like this, but Mayor Blackworth died Halloween night."

"I beg your pardon?" Elizabeth looked to Mrs. Potts to contradict my story.

"I'm so sorry," Mrs. Potts said.

"I don't understand."

"The sheriff is still figuring it out," I replied.

"What happened? Can you tell me anything?"

"I'm really not sure. I know he was found yesterday morning outside one of the village shops." I motioned with my hand in the general direction of Village Square, but it was impossible to see the location from where we stood, seeing it was clear across the lake. That didn't stop Elizabeth from craning her neck. "Perhaps someone inside the sheriff's department can help you?"

Elizabeth looked back over at the building once more. "He's dead. He's really dead." Elizabeth swayed on her feet, and I caught her elbow to steady her.

"Here, how about we have a seat." I looked behind me at the steps and debated lowering her to the ground here, but there was a bench up ahead off the sidewalk. "Can you walk?"

Elizabeth nodded.

We slowly made our way over to the park bench where Elizabeth sat down, and I took a seat beside her.

"I'm sorry. I must be in shock. I just can't believe it." Elizabeth held her head steady with her fingertips and massaged her temples.

"Can I get you anything?" I scanned both ends of the street. The business district didn't offer much in terms of refreshment, but there was a pharmacy not far up ahead. I could run in and grab Elizabeth a water or maybe something with sugar. Where was

Aunt Thelma when you needed her? I was sure she'd know a remedy or a spell for fainting.

"No, I'll be okay. Just let me sit for a moment."

I did just that, giving Elizabeth a minute to collect herself. I also noticed that Mrs. Potts was nowhere to be found. That was unfortunate, seeing I still wanted to talk to her about the other night. I had a feeling she wasn't done telling me the whole story.

I was still lost in my thoughts when Elizabeth turned to me and said, "It was murder, wasn't it. I can tell it's something awful by the look on your face."

I took a breath before answering. "It sounds like it, although the sheriff hasn't released many details."

"He told me what he was planning to do. I didn't believe him; I thought he was just ranting and raving like usual. I had no idea he was going to come over here and really wreak havoc, I promise you." Elizabeth's expression was filled with such guilt, I had no doubt that she was telling the truth.

"I don't think any of us believed it, not until he was caught by our own mayor that night."

Elizabeth hung her head in shame. "What am I going to do?" The question was rhetorical. I knew Elizabeth wasn't looking for an answer.

I sat with Elizabeth for another few minutes to make sure she was okay before standing up to excuse myself. "I'm actually on my way in to speak with the sheriff right now. Do you want to come in with me or have me—?"

"I think I'd like to stay here for a few more minutes," Elizabeth interrupted my offer to sit and wait longer with her.

I nodded. "Okay, well it was nice meeting you. I'm Angelica, by the way. Angelica Nightingale. My aunt owns the inn right around the bend if you find yourself needing a place to stay."

"Thank you so much."

I said my goodbyes and turned and jogged up the steps, hoping Vance would be inside and maybe have some answers.

FIFTEEN

Turns out, he wasn't. But he did call my cell phone back a few minutes later. I stepped outside to take the call, noticing that Elizabeth was no longer on the park bench either.

"What's going on?" Vance sounded out of breath.

"Were you running?"

"Yeah, the Enchanted Trail. I took Rocky for a run. Or more like he took me for a run." Vance's sentences came out in short, labored segments.

I knew I should've checked the trail. I chastised myself for being such a chicken. Next time, I'd trust my intuition and lace up my sneakers. "Listen, Sheriff Reynolds searched Clemmie's properties this morning and brought her in for questioning. She's refusing to cooperate until you're here."

"He's moving fast. Tell the sheriff I'm on my way."

"Will do."

I went back inside the station and tried to catch Deputy Jones' eye, but he was busy on his phone, his back turned to me. Everyone else seemed to be running all over the department, still processing paperwork and answering phone calls from Halloween night. I heard the words *evil scarecrow* and *devil spiders* repeated more than once.

I knew Clemmie was here somewhere, and I wanted a chance to talk with her or let her know that Vance would be here any minute.

Unfortunately, Amber was the one person who finally had a moment to assist me. Now, I know I'm not a defense attorney, or a prosecutor, or even a member of the sheriff's department, but for once, it would be nice for Amber to be kind.

"Can I help you?" Amber didn't even look up from her clipboard.

"Would it be possible to see Clemmie?"

"I'm sorry, she's here on official business. I can't let you speak to her right now." Amber was anything but apologetic as her eyes scrolled the papers before her.

"Can't or won't because I'm pretty sure it's not against the law. In fact, unless Clemmie's under arrest, you can't detain her." Heaven help me, but Amber got under my skin.

"Since when did you become a member of her legal counsel?"

I gritted my teeth.

"Since this morning." I looked over my shoulder as Vance strolled in through the front door.

"That was fast."

Vance flashed me a winning smile. "Benefit of living close by."

Amber's head snapped up in shock at Vance's remark, but she quickly found her snark. "No, she's not," she bit back.

"Are you privy to all of my business?" Vance cocked one eyebrow.

"No. I just meant that she's not an attorney."

"She doesn't have to be. She's part of my team. Isn't that right?" Vance turned his expression to me.

"Yes, yes it is." I looked back to Amber with a broad smile on my lips.

"Now, if you don't mind, I would like to have a word with my client. Unless you no longer plan on questioning her, and in that case, if you could send her out, that would be great."

"Oh no, she's still being questioned." Amber held her arm wide for us to accompany her to the other side of the reception desk. "She's in room number two. I'll tell my father you're here." Amber left Vance and I to continue the walk to the room alone.

"You're observant. Let me know if anything the sheriff says jumps out at you," Vance whispered to me while we walked.

"Took you long enough," Clemmie crossed her arms and glared at us when we walked in. In reality, less than an hour had passed between the first missed call and the moment we crossed the threshold, but I wasn't about to point that out.

Sheriff Reynolds didn't give us time to talk before he strolled in right after us.

"I see that we're all here now," Sheriff Reynolds did a double take at spotting me. I kept my expression neutral.

"Angie is working with me," Vance explained.

"Right, whatever. Let's get on with it then." Sheriff Reynolds took a baggie out from his back pocket and slapped it down on the table before flipping over one of the folding chairs so that it was facing backward. He straddled it as he sat.

"What do you make of this?" he asked Clemmie. His index finger tapping at the bag on the tabletop.

"I don't know. What is it? I don't have my glasses on." Clemmie leaned forward to examine the bag. It was full of light purple dried flowers.

"Wolfsbane. We found it in your tea shop." Sheriff Reynolds sat back, waiting for Clemmie's reaction.

"So? Wolfsbane's sold in half a dozen shops and can be found in twice as many homes. It's only a poison if you take too much of it."

"Half a dozen shops with people who had it out for Mayor Blackworth?"

"Given his antics night before last, I'd say so," Clemmie quipped.

"Now you listen here. We have you down for a motive and the means, and even the location puts the victim in your presence."

"Just because Blackworth's body was found in front of Clemmie's shop doesn't put her at the scene of the crime, Sheriff. You know that," Vance interjected.

Sheriff Reynolds shot Vance a look of annoyance. "Fine, can you tell me where you were Halloween night between the hours of eleven and midnight?"

"I was at home in my bed. Where else would you think I would be after the night I had had? What is the matter with you?"

Sheriff Reynolds was unfazed by Clemmie's scolding. "Can anyone confirm that?"

"You know I live alone."

"What you're saying is that you don't have an alibi."

"Sheriff, I'd wager she was where she was supposed to be. Ninety-nine percent of Silverlake was at home in bed."

"And you know that she doesn't have an alibi."

"And you know that the burden of proof falls on the prosecution, and right now you're grasping at straws."

Sheriff Reynolds grunted, pushed back from the table, and stood up. "I'm going to give you a minute to think about this. I was willing to strike a deal with you, but the longer you hold out, the less likely I am to be so kind. Think about that." The sheriff jabbed a finger in Clemmie's direction.

"Oh, I'll think about it all right," Clemmie grumbled.

"Unless you're arresting or detaining my client, we're through here." Vance stood to leave, and Clemmie and I followed suit.

I didn't say a word as I followed Vance out the door. Clemmie, on the other hand, had a hard time keeping her thoughts to herself. "That incompetent fool. Wolfsbane? You have to be kidding me. Thelma keeps wolfsbane in her kitchen."

"Sh-She does?" I looked over my shoulder while walking.

"Of course, any witch worth her salt does." Clemmie looked at me as if it were obvious.

"Er, right." Of course. How foolish of me, I thought sarcastically. Just when I thought I was getting the hang of being a witch, I was reminded how much I didn't know.

"Here's what I'm thinking. I want to go follow-up with Pete Sutherland." Vance said once we were outside once more.

"Get an alibi?" I asked.

"More or less and find out if anyone else from the maze was talking about revenge."

"Good idea. Mrs. Potts told me that she saw Chief Grady and Blackworth arguing in front of the tea shop Halloween night at eleven o'clock."

"And you're just now saying something?" Clemmie looked like she wanted to backhand me.

"But Blackworth was alive and well when the fire chief left him," I finished.

"Still, that's pretty big," Vance agreed with Clemmie

"I know. That's why I'm going to go talk to the fire chief while you go talk to Sutherland, and then we'll meet back up and compare notes. Sound good?"

"And while you two are doing that, I'm going to have myself a strong cup of tea. Maybe with a bit of Wolfsbane."

I raised my eyebrows. I didn't blame Clemmie for wanting a strong cup of tea, but I had no idea what Wolfsbane did and why she'd want to consume it. But I didn't doubt Clemmie when she said it was found throughout Silverlake.

After Clemmie walked away, I turned and looked at Vance. "Is it the assumption that Blackworth was poisoned with wolfsbane?"

"I guess so."

"Would that explain his blackened hand?"

"That I don't know. I'm not sure how the herb kills or what the symptoms are, but you can bet, that's one of the first things I'm going to look into.

"Okay, call me when you're done with Sutherland and we can research it together."

Vance and I parted ways, and I drove the short distance to the fire department.

Chief Grady was spraying off a line of firefighter boots covered with mud and hay from our Halloween maze when I walked up.

"That didn't take long." He let up the pressure on the hose nozzle and looked up at me. The fire chief looked like he hadn't yet slept in a week. He was sporting dark circles under his eyes and was in need of a good shave.

"Word travels fast in Silverlake. You know that."

"I heard they took Clemmie in for questioning. Doubt she's the murderer."

"What makes you so sure?" I played devil's advocate.

Chief Grady scrubbed the boots with a coarse-haired brush and soap, working up a good lather. "If Clemmie ever killed anyone, you wouldn't have to take her in for questioning. She'd proclaim it loud and clear from the center of Wishing Well Park."

I smirked. It shouldn't have been funny, but it was. "You're probably right."

I waited for the chief to finish scrubbing the last pair of boots and rinsing them off with the hose. When he was finished, he turned to me and said, "Mrs. Potts should have told you that Blackworth was alive and well when I walked away."

"Oh, she did." I was silent, letting my implications hang in the air.

"But that doesn't mean I didn't come back and finish him off."

"Is that what happened?" I cocked my head innocently to the side.

"You're good, I'll give you that. Might want to consider running for sheriff. But no, I left Blackworth and headed up to the hospital. I spent the night there. You can check with the staff. Kathy Sanders was the nurse. She'll confirm it."

"The hospital? Why, what happened?"

Chief Grady's jaw twitched in anger. I instinctively took a step back.

"My mother fell and broke her hip running away from one of Blackworth's spiders." The Fire Chief was barely able to control his rage. He balled his hand into a fist at his side and held it tight for a few seconds before slowly releasing it, his fingers extended straight with anger. "She's terrified of them. One jumped out at her from the bushes, and she couldn't escape it fast enough. She tripped over her porch steps and fell on the cement, shattering her hip in the process."

"I'm so sorry."

Chief Grady met my eyes. "Thank you." Some of his anger dissipated, but it was still there in his eyes waiting to erupt. "The thing is, though, I wanted Blackworth to pay. The man was a snake. He always had been, even when he was a kid."

"You knew him that long?"

"Unfortunately. I went to school with him and everything."

"I didn't know the Blackworth family was from Silverlake."

Chief Grady scoffed. "He wasn't known as Blackworth then. That's beside the point. The point is that I'm not sad to see he's dead, and I don't know what that says about me." Chief Grady closed his eyes and took a steadying breath.

I waited a minute for him to collect himself before asking a question that was weighing on my mind. "What do you think happened to him?"

"Your guess is as good as mine. A lot of people were angry with Blackworth that night. He cost thousands of dollars in damage and scared half the village." Chief Grady looked back at the firehouse. "My men are still exhausted, took all day yesterday to round up the bewitched decor, and frankly, I just hope they catch whoever murdered the man so we can put all of this behind us."

I agreed with Chief Grady. "I'll be thinking of you and your mom. If she needs anything, let me know."

Chief Grady replied with a nod. "She'll be in the hospital for another day or so. Constance gave her a bone mending potion, but it takes time to strengthen."

"Right, of course," was what I said. In reality, I was thinking, *What? A bone mending potion?* I had assumed Mrs. Grady would need to have her hip replaced. Second time in one day I was caught feeling like a mortal.

"Well, regardless, I hope you're able to get some sleep soon, and I'll see you around."

Chief Grady nodded once more, and I left him to get back to cleaning up.

SIXTEEN

When I left the fire station, I hadn't heard from Vance yet. I decided to kill two birds with one stone, go talk to Connie, and ask about curses and wolfsbane. I figured if any shop stocked the poison, it would be the potions shop, Mix it Up! Unlike the rest of the shops in Village Square, Mix it Up! looked immaculate outside and inside. The delinquents hadn't touched a single pumpkin on her sidewalk display, and from the looks of it, no pixies had entered either.

As I entered the shop, I spotted Connie working behind the counter like usual. A gold cauldron hung from the ceiling over a small blue flame. Rose-colored vapor drifted in the air, smelling like cotton candy. Connie sprinkled an unknown ingredient into the potion while her wand stirred the contents in smooth, even circles, all in its own.

"That smells good."

Connie glanced up and smiled before returning her attention back to the brew. "Good, it's supposed to."

"What is it?" I kept my distance. With Connie, you never knew what she was brewing, and it could be dangerous getting too close.

"Love potion. It's my biggest seller. But, from what I saw the other night, it looks like you don't need it." Connie looked up and winked.

One would think I'd be all blushed out, but it turns out, my cheeks still turned pink at the mention of me and Vance.

"It's good to see you two back together." Connie stated while blowing into the cauldron. A cloud of pink smoke rose into the air. Connie inhaled deeply and smiled in satisfaction. "Perfect," she declared. Thankfully, Connie then changed the subject. "So, seeing you're not here for a love potion, what can I do for you? Have you had a chance to break in your cauldron?"

"Not yet, but hopefully soon. I actually have two things I want to talk to you about, though."

"Oh yeah?" Connie pulled her wand out of the potion and surprisingly it was spotless. She then used the wand to extinguish the fire.

I watched the whole process, fascinated.

"What did you want to ask me?"

"Oh right. What do you know about wolfsbane?"

"Wolfsbane, the bane of wolves. Well, in the olden days, before witches and shifters got along, wolfsbane was used to kill or injure werewolves. Some shifters still use it to keep from transforming on a full moon, although you find that more in the mortal world where werewolves want to hide their true identities."

"So, just as the name implies."

"Exactly, but it's used in spell work too. It can destroy curses and blood oaths, break bindings, and alter memories. It's potent stuff. You've got to have your wits about you working with it because even handling it can get you killed."

"So why even use it in the first place?"

"Because sometimes you need potent stuff, and sometimes you just need to forget a really bad day."

"It can really erase your memory?" I knew memory charms existed, and I supposed it only made sense that there would be potions that could do the same. I'd just never heard of them.

"In a micro dose, yes. It can also give you the most amazing nap of your life."

"Interesting."

"Now, it's my turn to ask you a question. What do you need wolfsbane for?"

"Not me. Blackworth was poisoned with it. Sheriff Reynolds is trying to pin it on Clemmie since she sells the leaves in her tea shop."

"As do I."

"That's what I assumed. Clemmie said that half a dozen shops in Village Square carried it."

"It does have practical uses if you know what you're doing." Connie thought for a moment. "I'm just glad that Blackworth didn't make it through my wards because then I would be a suspect."

"What's that?"

"Someone set off my wards Halloween night around nine o'clock. I'd bet money that it was Blackworth seeing how he set pixies loose in Clemmie's shop and released tarantulas in the apothecary."

"Oh my gosh." That was putting my thoughts mildly. I don't know what I would've done if I'd arrived at Clemmie's and seen tarantulas crawling everywhere. I shuddered at the thought and couldn't help scanning the floor to make sure there wasn't anything creepy crawling my way. "Is there a way to find out if it was Blackworth?"

"Did one of his hands turn black?" Connie asked.

My jaw dropped. "How did you know?"

"It's the mark of a thief. It doesn't wash off either, but instead fades over time. I thought it was pretty brilliant."

I instantly thought that I had to let Vance know. I almost left right then and there when I remembered Eleanor. "Oh, one more thing. We figured out Aunt Velma's curse. Not sure if you heard about Luke's nieces, but they were the ones to blame for the croaking. But I also learned about another Silverlake resident who's been cursed."

"Another curse? Who?"

"Bonnie Daniels' great, great, Aunt Eleanor."

"Who now?"

"She's a ghost at the tavern. She lives upstairs." I went on to relate Eleanor's story, hoping Bonnie wouldn't be mad at me for telling her family's history. She never said to keep quiet, but I found it telling that recent generations of Silverlake residents didn't know much about it. I also told Connie my theory about Tabitha cursing an heirloom or the tavern itself.

"Both of them are possible, although the jewelry makes the most sense. And I'd bet money it's a piece from Oscar's side of the family, that way Tabitha could ensure that the curse would remain in effect."

"Why not the tavern?" Maybe it was just wishful thinking on my part. But it would be a whole lot easier to break a curse on the tavern than to find a piece of jewelry that might not even exist anymore.

"Because how could Tabitha be sure that Eleanor's family would still own the tavern property? For all Tabitha knew, Eleanor's family could've moved to India."

"Good point." I twisted my face in concentration. "That does make it harder," I confessed.

"True. But if you do find the piece of jewelry, or

suspect you have, bring it to me, and I'll see what I can do."

"That's a big if, but thank you."

Fresh from my conversation with Connie, I headed right to the tavern. I wanted a chance to talk with Eleanor and also grab a bite to eat. I was starving. I looked at my phone and saw that Vance still hadn't called, which was perfectly all right. I had things to do and places to go.

Craig was behind the bar today, and he greeted me when I walked in. "Hey Angelica, looking for Percy?"

Craig's question caught me off guard. "Er, sure." Percy was probably with Eleanor, so in a way, I guess I was looking for the ghost.

"He and the misses are upstairs. Go ahead, and head on up." Craig motioned with his thumb behind him.

I had never been through the tavern's kitchen, let alone upstairs. I had no idea where I was going. "Through the kitchen then?"

"Straight back, you can't miss the staircase."

"Got it."

If any of the workers wondered what I was up to, they didn't say a thing as I made my way through the kitchen and toward the back as Craig had instructed. I nodded my head at the line cook. I couldn't remember his name, he was a year or two out of high school and a friend of Emily's who would be just finishing up her shift at the inn. I walked like I knew where I was going and was happy when I spotted a staircase in the back left corner that only went up. The orange glow of a single bulb shown from above.

I side-stepped stacked boxes of empty beer bottles and took the steps one at a time. The stairs were narrow and worn with age. The dark stain was only visible on the edges of the steps, which creaked as I ascended. The sound made my presence known before I appeared at the top of the landing, which opened into a sitting room. A fireplace with large, smooth round stones for the hearth served as a focal point. I realized it lined up perfectly with the wood-fire pizza oven downstairs. A writing desk sat on the opposite wall in front of the window, which was where Percy was sitting, pouring over a book of some sort. Bonnie and Eleanor stood behind him.

"Those are all the dates we've tried." Bonnie leaned forward, her finger trailing the text. "On her birthday, death day, the day she called off the wedding, Oscar's birthday, the day Tabitha died, Halloween, All Soul's Day. Pretty much any important day the family could think of."

Eleanor turned and winked at me. I instantly smiled in response.

"Hope I'm not interrupting," I said by way of introduction.

Percy glanced over his shoulder, but he didn't

acknowledge me. He was too engrossed in the book and what Bonnie was saying.

"Angelica, how are you?" Bonnie whirled around.

"Good. I'm glad you guys are all here. I too wanted to talk about the curse."

"Did you figure it out?" Percy's eyes widened with excitement.

"Maybe?" I couldn't keep the hesitation from my voice. "It's more like I wanted to ask a couple questions that might help me figure it out. I had talked to Connie yesterday about curses when my aunt was croaking, and I went back and chatted with her for a bit today. I hope that's okay." I looked to Bonnie and then Eleanor. Neither one of them seemed to object. "I wasn't sure if it was a secret."

"No, it's not a secret," Eleanor said.

"More like we gave up trying to break it," Bonnie explained.

"Okay, well Connie had suggested to me when Aunt Thelma was croaking that maybe a cursed piece of jewelry was to blame. Have you guys explored that angle?" Bonnie and Eleanor looked at one another as they tried to recall everything they had tried.

Bonnie took the thick volume from Percy and began to flip through the pages. The heavy book was made of brown leather, and the pages looked thin and transparent.

"Let's see, we explored if the tavern itself was

cursed, but we ruled that out. Then, my great, great, great uncle, that would be Eleanor's father, had left a painting to the family, but that wasn't cursed either."

"As for jewelry, we don't have much. I have my mother's wedding ring, but I had that long before I ever met Oscar."

"Oh?" I wondered how that came to be.

"My mother died when I was a little girl," Eleanor clarified.

"I'm sorry to hear that." I didn't think I could feel any sorrier for the ghost, and yet here I was feeling heartbroken yet once again.

"That's okay, she comes to visit quite often," Eleanor said with a smile.

I opened my mouth to speak but then shut it. Having nothing to add to the conversation.

"What was that look for?" Bonnie asked me.

"It's nothing. Just thinking like a mortal again."

"It'll trip you up every time," Bonnie laughed.

I brought the conversation back around to the curse. "You don't think there's any way Tabitha could've gotten her hand on your mother's ring, do you? It would be the perfect thing to curse, she'd know you'd never get rid of it."

"I don't see how. I never took it off." Eleanor retrieved the ring from a gold chain around her neck. The image was transparent and blue like Eleanor, indicating that she had been wearing the piece when she died.

I furrowed my brow, the ring was just the sort of heirloom I'd been hoping to find, but if Eleanor was sure it was curse free, I wasn't sure what I could do about it.

"Is the physical piece here somewhere?" I looked to Bonnie.

"I have it at my house. Aunt Eleanor didn't like keeping it here at the tavern. Too many people milling about."

"Can't tell you how many drunk patrons have found their way up those stairs over the years," Eleanor added.

I grimaced at the awful prospect. "Do you think it would be all right if I had Connie take a look at it anyway? She offered to help."

Again, the two ladies shared a look before Eleanor said, "I don't have a problem with it. Take good care of it, won't you?"

"Of course, or Bonnie, do you want to meet me at Mix it Up! when you have a moment?" I liked that plan better versus having a precious family heirloom in my possession.

"I can do that."

I then switched gears.

"What about Oscar's family? What was his last name?"

"Weaver," Eleanor said.

"You said they've been helpful before; any chance they might be again? I'm wondering if maybe

Tabitha cursed one of her own family's heirlooms. It would ensure that it would be passed down from generation to generation and the curse would remain unbroken."

"Of all the rotten things to do." Percy scowled. It was the first time he had spoken up during my visit.

"That sounds like Tabitha," Eleanor's voice sounded distant and sad. Her gaze was fixed down at the carpet.

"Only problem is, it seems like the Weavers dropped off the face of the earth," Bonnie said.

"Like magically disappeared?" I was proud of myself for thinking like a witch for once. It was much easier for magical families to disappear when we could slip into enchanted villages like Silverlake.

"No, like the family name seems to have died out with the last generation. The last Weaver passed away two years ago," Eleanor said.

"And yet the curse still remains." I couldn't deny that that fact took a little bit of wind out of my sails. "Well, let's take your mother's ring to Connie and see what she thinks." I had a feeling Eleanor's ring wasn't the answer, but maybe it would bring us one step closer.

SEVENTEEN

I forgot how hungry I was until I stepped outside of the tavern, and my stomach growled. Maybe solving these mysteries was going to be the death of me.

Vance chose that moment to ring my cell phone.

"Hey, I'm just finishing up. Do you still want to meet up?" he asked.

"Yeah, how about the cafe? I'm starving." This time I meant it. I wasn't going anywhere else until I filled my belly. Sleuthing on an empty stomach never ended well.

"I'll meet you there."

It only took me a handful of minutes to snake my way over to the cafe. Like the tavern, the cafe was located in Village Square. It was one of three dining establishments the shopping district offered with the tavern and the Simmering Spoon being the other two.

"There's my girl!" Vance's mom said to me when I walked through the door. Heather swooped in for a one-armed hug. "I was hoping you'd stop by." Heather then bent low as if she were imparting a secret, "There's power in forgiving, you know. Thank you for forgiving my son," she whispered in my ear and gave me a squeeze.

I couldn't reply. I was too overcome with emotions. Instead, I found myself simply nodding. I might have murmured an "of course," but I couldn't be certain.

"My son meeting you?" Heather's voice was back to being light and carefree.

"He'll be here in a few minutes."

"Go ahead and have that corner booth. I'll be by with that peach tea in a minute." I nodded my thanks and grabbed two laminated menus from the hostess stand as I weaved my way through the crowded cafe to the back booth, which was usually reserved for parties of six or more. I wasn't even sure why I even bothered with the menus. I always ordered the exact same thing, which was a Montecristo sandwich and seasoned fries, and Vance knew his mom's menu by heart.

As promised, Heather dropped off a large peach iced tea and Vance slid in the booth a few moments later. He leaned forward and planted a quick peck on my cheek before settling into place. "I've been wanting to do that for months."

"Stop," I said with a smile. I wasn't going to lie; Vance's show of affection sent butterflies fluttering in my tummy, making me feel like I was sixteen again, and I liked it. It was a feeling I hadn't experienced with anyone else all those years in between. To me, that spoke volumes.

"What did you find out?" I got right to it.

Vance poked his straw out of the paper and slipped it into his coke. "Nothing good. I talked to Dr. Fitz. He smelled the poison on Blackworth at the scene. It was spilled on his clothes along with tea."

"Clemmie didn't do it."

"I know that. She knows that. But who else would've slipped Blackworth wolfsbane-laced tea? It doesn't look good."

I chewed my bottom lip. "I know."

I tried to look at the case from a rational stand-point. Vance was right, it didn't look good. On one hand, I'd swear up and down Clemmie was innocent, but on the other hand, what if Clemmie had been inside her shop when she saw Chief Grady and Blackworth arguing? It would've been easy for her to invite him inside and poison him. I was almost scared to share my thoughts out loud. As if speaking the words would somehow make them come true.

"What did Chief Grady have to say?"

Vance's question snapped me out of my thoughts.

"Oh man, I feel so bad for him. Mrs. Grady tripped and broke her hip trying to run away from one of Blackworth's spiders."

Vance's face was frozen in horror. Mrs. Grady wasn't the only one who hated spiders. "Sounds like a motive to me, and he was at the scene."

"Except Mrs. Potts said Chief Grady walked away from Blackworth, and the chief has an alibi. He left Village Square to head up to the hospital and sit with his mom all night. I haven't checked his alibi yet, but I'll be shocked if the nurse doesn't confirm it."

Vance sighed. "Then we're back to square one?"

"Looks like it." Vance and I didn't talk much about the case once our food arrived. We were both too hungry to do much talking at all.

After half of my food was gone, I remembered my conversation with Connie. "Oh! I forgot to tell you. I found out why Blackworth's hand was black. It was from Connie's wards. He tried breaking into her place around nine that night."

"So, it's not the twins."

"No, thank heavens. I still need to tell Luke. Let me send him a text right now." I did just that before I forgot again. I then switched and thought about my conversation with Mrs. Potts earlier. "You know, I don't think Mrs. Potts had finished telling me her story. Blackworth's assistant appeared and interrupted her." I told Vance about Elizabeth. "I think it would be smart if we paid our old teacher visit. What do you think?"

"And maybe Elizabeth. Sounds like she knows more about Blackworth than any of us."

"You're right. We're assuming that it was someone in Silverlake that killed him, but it could easily have been someone from Harrisville that followed him over here."

"Maybe even Elizabeth herself."

"Gosh, don't say that. I really like her, and she seemed genuinely shocked to hear about Blackworth."

"Or that's what she wants you to think."

I gulped and prayed Vance wasn't right. I'd invited her to stay at the inn that night. The thought of a murderer staying under the same roof as me and my aunt sent shivers down my arms.

After Vance and I finished eating, we set out to talk to our old teacher. Mrs. Potts was sitting in the rocking chair on her front porch staring off into space when Vance and I pulled in front of her house. The poor woman didn't even look up.

"This doesn't look good," Vance muttered to me as we got out of his truck.

I agreed that it didn't.

"Mrs. Potts, is everything okay?" Vance asked as we approached the driveway.

Mrs. Potts didn't respond. Instead, she chose to stare wide-eyed at some fixed point in the distance.

"You think she's been spelled?" Vance kept his voice low.

I shrugged my shoulders in response. It wasn't the first time I'd questioned Mrs. Potts' sanity today.

"Mrs. Potts?" I tried again as we walked up to the porch.

Finally, when we were about two feet from her, Mrs. Potts acknowledged us, snapping out of her reverie. The older woman turned and looked at us and said as plain as day, "I think I killed him."

"Who? Blackworth?" Vance looked to me, but I shook my head as if to say I have no idea.

"I didn't mean to. It was an accident. I don't even know how it happened." Mrs. Potts wouldn't meet our eyes.

I took a seat on the porch steps while Vance leaned against the porch's railing.

"I can't explain it, but I know it's my fault." Mrs. Potts looked to us for answers, but neither one of us knew how she'd reached her conclusion.

"Maybe if you go back to our conversation earlier. You told me Chief Grady walked away from Blackworth. Did something happen after that?" I asked helpfully.

Mrs. Potts looked at me somberly and nodded. I didn't think she was going to speak for the longest time, but finally she opened her mouth and said, "I approached Gerry, that's how I knew him when he was a little boy, Gerry Webb, and invited him over for tea."

"Did you say Webb?" I hadn't planned on interrupting Mrs. Potts, but I didn't know Blackworth's real surname was Webb. I turned to Vance. "That's Elizabeth's last name."

"His assistant?"

I nodded.

"She didn't tell you they were related?"

I shook my head. Vance and I shared a look that said how odd we thought that fact to be.

"Sorry, I didn't mean to interrupt," I said to Mrs. Potts.

"That's okay. I was just saying how Gerry was always such a troublemaker, even when he was in my class, but I never give up on a student, ever. Even Gerry. Right to the end, I tried to reach him. Get him to see the error of his ways, you know?"

Both Vance and I nodded that we understood. I fought the urge to interrupt again, as I hadn't known that Mrs. Potts was Mayor Blackworth's, or Gerry Webb's if you will, teacher, but then I remembered Chief Grady had said something about being in school with Blackworth, and it all made sense.

"And it was working. Gerry came over and agreed to a cup of tea. Before the water even boiled, he was spilling all of his past deeds. Every person he'd ever bewitched. Every curse he'd ever cast. You name it. It was as if the flood gates had opened, and

Gerry confessed all of his sins." Mrs. Potts stared off into the distance again as if she was recalling the scene. This time Vance and I waited for Mrs. Potts to continue.

"Then, let me see, I'm trying to recall what happened. I remember pouring the tea and slipping off into the kitchen for some shortbread. I had just baked it that morning out of the Enchanting Appetizers cookbook. You know which one I'm talking about?" Mrs. Potts' question was directed to me. This past summer I'd helped her pick out a winning cookbook for her cooking club, and she was constantly thanking me.

I nodded that I remembered and encouraged her to continue.

"I came back out, and Gerry excused himself to use the restroom. When he came back, he was very different. I can't explain it, but it was like the Gerry from two minutes before was gone, and all that was left was this hardened, angry man." Mrs. Potts' eyes filled with unshed tears. She took a moment to compose herself, taking a deep breath in and out and then cleared her throat. "He waited while I drank my tea. Just sitting there, watching me. I can't explain it, it was almost as if he was smirking at me. It gave me the chills, I tell you. Look at my arms. There's goosebumps rising right up on them." Mrs. Potts held out her arm for us to see. "Then when I was done, he downed his tea in one gulp and walked out the door without even saying goodbye." Mrs. Potts rubbed her shoulders with her hands as if trying to warm up.

"And why do you think you killed him?" Vance asked gently.

"Well, who else could've done it? He drank tea at my house and was found dead minutes later. It's all over the news."

I hadn't seen the local news, but that didn't surprise me. Silverlake reporters would be chomping at the bit to cover the story. It might even be big enough to warrant a visit from Starry Evans, Witch News Network's lead anchor. I really didn't want to see that happen after we'd worked so hard with the fall festival to restore Silverlake's reputation.

Mrs. Potts was starting to get frantic.

While Vance worked to calm down our former teacher, parts of the puzzle began to snap into place. I had a theory as to what had happened, but I needed to talk to Dr. Fitz first.

Finally, I stood and knew what we needed to do. "Come on, Mrs. Potts. We have a field trip to take."

Vance raised his brows at me expectantly.

"You're taking me to the sheriff, aren't you?" Mrs. Potts' words were a mere whisper.

"No, I'm taking you to see Dr. Fitz. I'm hoping he has the answers."

EIGHTEEN

Dr. Fitz was one of only two private practice doctors in Silverlake. The rest worked at the small community hospital, many of them trained healers versus medical doctors. I had no idea if Dr. Fitz would be in his office, but I thought that would be the best place to look first, not to mention more pleasant than the village morgue.

Vance and Mrs. Potts waited in the car while I ran inside to see if the doctor was available. Much to my surprise, the man himself was standing behind the reception desk, conversing with one of his nurses. Both Dr. Fitz and the nurse looked up when I walked in.

"Angelica, this is a surprise," the aging werewolf said with a smile. I couldn't help but notice that his canines seemed a bit elongated and then I remembered the full moon had just been the other night. I wondered if the doctor had been out running under the full moon. The mental image was unnerving as I pictured the doctor as himself running on four legs through the trees wearing his lab coat and stethoscope versus as a fully formed wolf. I shook my head at the bizarre image and got back to the point of my visit.

"Hi Dr. Fitz."

"Is everything okay? Yesterday's discovery probably gave you quite a scare."

"Oh, no. I'm okay, but that is what I wanted to talk to you about. Do you have a minute to speak with me, Vance, and Mrs. Potts?"

Both the nurse and Dr. Fitz looked over my shoulder as if expecting the other two individuals to materialize behind me. "They're waiting in the car."

Dr. Fitz looked at his gold wristwatch. I had a feeling the doctor avoided silver at all costs. "I have about fifteen minutes. Will that work?"

"Yes, I appreciate it. Let me go tell the other two." I walked back out of the waiting room and opened the front door, waving at Vance to come in.

Within a few minutes, we were settled in the good doctor's office. Dr. Fitz's office may have been high-fashion forty years ago, but it hadn't been updated since. His desk was light oak like the accordion blinds on the window, and the table that ran behind his desk. The table was stacked with medical textbooks and framed photos of loved ones. A gold nameplate sat on the desk along with a matching pen set that looked as if it was never used if the dust on them was any indication.

"Here, have a seat." Dr. Fitz motioned to the two leather chairs that stood on the opposite side of his desk while he took up residence in the coordinating one on his side. "Sorry, I only have two chairs."

"That's okay, I can stand," Vance pulled back the chair for Mrs. Potts to sit in and went to do the same for me, but I had already sat down.

"So, what's this about?" Dr. Fitz's eyes looked to each one of us in turn.

"I'm not quite sure," Mrs. Potts said, her voice wobbling as she turned to me to elucidate the matter.

"I'll explain." I had kept my suspicions vague as we drove the short distance to the doctor's office. There was a chance I was wrong, and I didn't want to get Mrs. Potts' hopes up in case I was. "Sheriff Reynolds told us that Mayor Blackworth was poisoned with wolfsbane-laced tea."

"It was on the news too," Mrs. Potts interrupted.

"Right," I agreed with Mrs. Potts.

"That was my preliminary finding, but there has been a bit of a breakthrough." At the doctor's words, my eyebrows shot up, and Vance leaned forward. Even Mrs. Potts seemed on the edge of her seat. "But I'm afraid that information hasn't been released yet, and I'm not at liberty to discuss the case with you."

Mrs. Potts deflated.

Vance looked to me as if to say: Now what?

I took a chance. "Is the breakthrough that you found wolfsbane in Mayor Blackworth's possession?" I asked hesitantly.

"Why, yes. How did you know?" It was Dr. Fitz's turn to be eager for information.

The doctor's words were the confirmation that I needed. I turned to Mrs. Potts. "Did you switch cups with Mayor Blackworth by chance?" It was the only thing that made sense.

Mrs. Potts mouth mimicked speaking, opening and closing, but no sound came out for a moment. Eventually she said, "That's right, I did. I didn't think anything of it, but when Gerry excused himself for a moment, I noticed I had served him my favorite teacup, and I switched it before either one of us took a drink. It was silly of me really, but I am awfully fond of that cup."

Vance picked up on my train of thought. "You're saying Blackworth poisoned Mrs. Potts' teacup and inadvertently ended up ingesting the poison when she switched the cups."

"Exactly." I gave a curt nod.

"I'll be." The good doctor was rendered speech-less as he sat back in his chair and thought the case through.

"Poison me, but why?" Mrs. Potts had yet to put everything together.

"It was something you said that helped me figure

it out. You said that Mayor Blackworth confessed all of his sins to you, and then something in him snapped right? Like he suddenly looked a bit sinister after you came back with the shortbread." That wasn't the word Mrs. Potts had used, but fit the vision she had painted.

"That's right," Mrs. Potts confirmed.

"I think he poisoned you to cover his tracks. He couldn't have someone knowing everything he'd done. It's like what Elizabeth told me." I turned and looked up at Vance. "She said that she always had to clean up his messes, but I bet even she doesn't know the half of it. Blackworth did a lot of wrong things in his life, and he couldn't have one person knowing all of his misdeeds."

"So, he accidentally killed himself," Vance surmised.

"That's what I think. Is that possible, doctor?"

Dr. Fitz was thoughtful for a moment. "That very well could be how it happened. Blackworth had enough wolfsbane on him to kill ten people. It's why I could smell it so strongly."

"Do you still have the teacup from that night?" I should've asked Mrs. Potts earlier.

"I do. Normally I'd wash the set and put it away, but I was so out of sorts when he left, that it's still sitting in the kitchen. I can't even bring myself to look at it."

"That should prove it then," Vance said.

Both Dr. Fitz and I agreed with him.

"So, I didn't kill him?" Mrs. Potts looked at me wide-eyed. Her eyes glistened with tears.

I touched my hand to her knee to comfort her. "No, you didn't. Blackworth has no one to blame but himself."

Mrs. Potts exhaled a rush of air, and then she cried. It was hard to tell if they were tears of relief or grief for Mayor Blackworth's decisions. Dr. Fitz handed her a box of tissues as I comforted my former teacher the best that I could.

"I can't explain how I feel. I kept thinking I was to blame. I didn't know how, but I felt like it was all my fault."

"For what it's worth, I never thought you were to blame, even when you did."

Mrs. Potts took my hand and gave it a squeeze. "I always did like you, Angelica. You too, Vance," she looked up and over her shoulder. She sniffed. "I'm so happy you two are back together."

The comment was so unexpected that I couldn't help but laugh. "Me too, Mrs. Potts. Me too."

An hour later I was leaving the sheriff's department after sitting with Mrs. Potts while she gave her statement. Amber hadn't wanted to hear the truth, but Deputy Jones was more than agreeable. He didn't waste any time sending a unit to Mrs. Potts' house to fetch the tea set, agreeing that Blackworth had most likely accidentally killed himself.

Vance had to run back to the office to write up contracts for the Robertsons. It turns out that the boys were responsible for damaging Village Square and the parents were agreeing to pay retribution to all the shop owners and residents in return for them not pressing charges.

"I heard there's been news." I turned at the source of the voice. Elizabeth was walking briskly down the sidewalk toward me.

"They may have solved the case," I replied once we met face-to-face.

"Will you just tell me? I hate to have to talk to that awful Amber woman if I don't have to."

I felt for Elizabeth. I never wanted to talk to Amber if I didn't have to either, but I wasn't sure if it was my place to impart the news. Not to mention it still needed to be confirmed.

"Please."

It was just one simple word. And the one thing Elizabeth could've said to get me to tell her the truth. I sighed. "We don't know for sure yet, but it looks like it was an accident. We think Mayor Blackworth was trying to poison Mrs. Potts, his second-grade teacher, when she switched the teacups, and he drank it instead."

I wasn't sure how Elizabeth would handle the news, knowing that her cousin had tried to kill his teacher, but relief flooded her eyes. "That's so awful, and yet I'm not surprised." Elizabeth brushed away a stray tear that trailed her cheek and she sniffed, trying to keep her emotions in check. "Blackworth always used magic for what he wanted. He cursed and spelled people left and right. I always knew it would catch up with him someday. I just didn't know it would be this tragic."

"Why didn't you tell me you were related?"

"Would you claim him as a relation? In all honesty, I would've washed my hands of him years ago if I hadn't promised my aunt on her deathbed that I'd keep an eye on him. I was the only family he had left. I hope Aunt Tammy realizes that I tried, but there was no keeping Gerry in check. That was his real name, Gerry Webb."

"I know."

Elizabeth heaved a sigh. After a moment she said, "I guess I still need to go in there. I've been thinking about what to tell the people of Hendersonville. I need to talk to Sheriff Reynolds and see if he'll agree to a coverup of sorts."

The sheriff would have to. You couldn't tell mortals what had really happened.

"I guess you do. I'll leave you to it, then. Will I be seeing you later?"

Elizabeth nodded. "I've already made my reservation. I figure it will take a day or two to figure this all out."

"Okay, I'll catch up with you then. I think tonight is movie night, maybe it will help take your mind off things?" When we had renovated the inn, Aunt Thelma and I were adamant about keeping the property's old-world charm. We wanted a destination where people could still find the classic family vacations they used to love, only with the modern amenities of today. Hence, a classic movie on the patio brought to you curtsy of wi-fi and a projector.

"Maybe," Elizabeth looked unsure, and I didn't blame her. It would take more than a movie to help settle her nerves. Her unease had me thinking I should stop by Connie's and see if she would whip up a calming potion to help settle the poor woman's mind.

When Elizabeth and I parted ways, I headed to Mix it Up! to do just that.

NINETEEN

"I can't believe you figured it out, dear." Aunt Thelma and I were passing out bags of popcorn to our hotel guests. The opening credits of Gone With The Witch began and we side stepped tables to move out of the way.

"I'm just glad no one in Silverlake is to blame." Aunt Thelma and I stood off to the side while she worked to adjust the volume on the laptop.

"Here, let me help." Aunt Thelma and technology didn't mix. It took me a couple clicks on the computer, and I stepped back to see how it all looked and sounded on the big white screen facing the lake. A blanket of stars was the backdrop.

"Now if I could only track down Oscar Weaver's family and solve Eleanor's curse," I whispered, keeping my voice soft so I wouldn't bother our guests.

"Did you say Weaver?" Elizabeth had chosen that moment to step outside and join us.

"That's right," Aunt Thelma said.

"That's my family's last name, or it was until my grandmother changed it to Webb."

"What?" I practically shouted. Several heads whipped my way. "Sorry," I mouthed and then turned my attention to Elizabeth, motioning for her follow me into the lobby so that we weren't being inconsiderate to those watching the movie.

"What about this name change?"

"It was before I was born, but Gran changed it to honor our family's witchy heritage, among other reasons." Given what I knew of the Weaver's family history, I wasn't surprised. "It's not like we were attached to the Weaver name or anything, and I guess the names Weaver and Webb were used inter-changeably back in the day as an occupational name for a weaver, which my ancestors were. Plus, Webb sounds more witchy, doesn't it?"

"It does and it explains why the Weaver line disappeared a generation ago," I said.

Elizabeth nodded. "Gran wouldn't talk about it, but Aunt Tammy said something about saving the family legacy, too. I asked what she meant, but she wouldn't say."

"I might be able to help there. What do you know about Tabitha Weaver?"

Elizabeth licked her lips nervously. "I know a little, not much. But I know she was powerful."

I went on to explain Tabitha's curse and how Eleanor was still trapped at the tavern all these years later. "So, you see, I'm wondering if you have a family heirloom, something that Tabitha may have cursed?"

"I do have something. I never thought it might be cursed." With trembling fingers, Elizabeth hooked the gold chain from around her neck and pulled it forward, revealing a star-shaped locket. It was silver and quarter-sized with a small ruby in the middle. "It actually belonged to Tabitha. I never heard anything about the curse. My aunt gave it to me on the day she died. Made me promise to keep it with me always. I never thought it could be tied to something so awful. Aunt Tammy didn't say." Elizabeth looked racked with guilt.

"She probably didn't know." Truthfully, I had no idea what Tammy Webb knew, but it seemed like the right thing to say.

"I hope you're right."

I hoped I was right, too. "Does that mean that Blackworth was Tabitha's great, great grandson?"

Elizabeth confirmed my question with a nod.

I looked to Elizabeth as the gravity of the realization began to sink in. "This necklace might be it, and if it is, we might be able to break two curses tonight."

"Two? I don't understand."

"Eleanor's and the one that hangs over your

family. Because one thing I've learned is that you can't cause that much heartache and trouble without it coming back to you tenfold. I think your family has seen that firsthand."

Again, Elizabeth nodded.

"What do you say? Are you willing to try?"

"I'm willing to try anything."

I knew Eleanor's history. I knew that her family had tried to break the curse on Eleanor's birthday, Halloween, and a hundred dates in-between. I knew they'd all but given up hope. But this time, I was praying that hope would come roaring back to life on an unremarkable Sunday evening in November.

The tavern was slow, which was usual for a Sunday night. All the tourists had driven home from holiday weekend, and all that remained were the locals. And after the busy holiday weekend and unexpected cleanup, it was safe to say, we were all tired.

But this was too important to wait.

Bonnie's eyebrows drew together when she saw us walk in. She had been talking to Carl at the end of the bar but patted the countertop and left him to meet me and Elizabeth at the opposite end.

"We might have found it," I said without preamble.

"Are you sure?"

"No. But this is Elizabeth. She's a descendant of Tabitha's."

"Say no more. Hang on a minute." Bonnie disappeared into the kitchen for a moment. We heard her call for Craig a second later, asking him to keep an eye out front before motioning for me and Elizabeth to follow her back.

"It's okay," I told Elizabeth reading the apprehension on her face. "Eleanor is really nice."

"But what if you're wrong, and this isn't it?" Elizabeth hissed.

"Then it's not your fault, and we'll keep looking." I gave Elizabeth a level stare. I couldn't force her to hand over her heirloom, and I wasn't expecting her to. I was mostly hoping to introduce Elizabeth to Eleanor and that together we could brainstorm a spell or even a potion to break the curse. Maybe it would even involve wolfsbane as Connie had said it was used to break curses and blood oaths. And if that was the case, you could bet I'd leave the potion-making up to Connie. Her shop was closed for the night, but I'd get her opinion first thing tomorrow.

"Isn't this a surprise. What are you all doing tonight?" Eleanor asked when the three of us filed in upstairs. She was sitting by the fire reading. I wondered how many nights the ghost had sat in that same chair reading a book, and how many books she'd been able to read in the span of two lifetimes plus the one she had lived. It was mindboggling.

"It might not be anything, but this is Elizabeth.

She's Tabitha's great, great niece." I looked to Elizabeth to make sure I had gotten that right.

"How's that possible?" Eleanor asked, clearly confused.

"My family's last name was Weaver until my grandma changed it to Webb."

"Isn't that something," Eleanor said with feeling.

"I don't know much about Tabitha. My mom and aunt didn't talk about her much. From what I gathered, it was a sore subject and I was too scared to ask. But after talking to Angelica, I think I know the real reason why my grandmother changed our last name." Elizabeth quickly explained, the words rushing out. "I didn't know about the curse. I never suspected anything, I promise you. I kept the locket because my aunt said it was important, and I pray that even she didn't know why. Aunt Tammy didn't have a mean bone in her body." Elizabeth took a shaky breath. It was clear she was on the verge of crying.

"It's okay," Eleanor replied, trying to calm the woman down. Even in her imprisonment, Eleanor still didn't blame Elizabeth, the one woman who may have been able to break her curse years ago if she'd only known she existed.

"It's not okay. From what Angelica's told me, this isn't something I wish to keep." Elizabeth unclasped the locket around her neck.

"A Weaver family heirloom." Bonnie was unable to keep the hope from her voice.

Elizabeth nodded. "It's yours to keep. If it will help you in any way, I want you to have it." Elizabeth lowered herself onto her knees and placed the necklace in Eleanor's palm, closing it with her own. "I'm so sorry my family cursed you. What Tabitha did to you was despicable, and I'll do whatever it takes to set you free. You have my word."

In that instant, power erupted in the room. I felt it move through my body like an electric current. Blinding white light shot out from the locket. I threw my arm up to shield my face and turned away from the source. A rush of warm wind blew about the room, rippling paper, and sending my hair blowing back. Somebody gasped, it might have even been me.

Then, like a lightning bolt, it was over.

The room dimmed, and the air stilled.

I slowly lowered my arm and looked around the room. Everything was exactly the same, and yet it wasn't.

No one spoke for a minute. We were all too stunned to move, let alone speak.

Then Eleanor found her voice. "Can it be? Am I really free to go?" Her voice trembled with emotion.

"Could it have been that simple?" Elizabeth asked me.

"I don't know." None of us knew the answer to that question.

"Only one way to find out." Bonnie held her arm

out, and I saw that it was shaking, mirroring how I felt on the inside.

A mixture of nerves and excitement filled the room as Eleanor cautiously peered down the steps.

She looked back to us.

I nodded encouragingly.

"Go on, it'll be alright." Bonnie tried to sound confident, but I could tell she was just as nervous as the rest of us.

Slowly, Eleanor walked down the stairs. One agonizing step at a time. I prayed this was it. I hadn't planned on breaking the curse tonight, but after what had transpired upstairs, I'd be crushed if Eleanor was still a prisoner to the tavern. I couldn't imagine how she'd feel.

I wondered if anything like this had ever happened before. Had Eleanor ever tasted freedom, but at the last minute had it snatched away? I was too afraid to ask.

At the bottom of the steps, Eleanor looked over her shoulder, as if questioning whether this could really be happening.

I held my breath and crossed my fingers it would work. I looked over and saw that Elizabeth was doing the same.

The walk to the back door took an eternity.

"Craig, come quick!" Bonnie yelled.

Eleanor had bypassed the front of the house and was making her way out the back door to the kitchen.

I didn't know the limits of the curse, whether Eleanor had ever been able to step outside or not, but by the looks on everyone's faces, I had a feeling the answer had been no.

"What is it?" Craig poked his head into the kitchen. His eyes widened. He looked too shocked to move. I knew exactly how he felt.

Eleanor reached the back door.

Painfully and slowly, she reached her hand out for the knob, taking a deep breath that her body hadn't needed for two hundred years. She turned the knob and stepped out into the nighttime air.

I can't explain the joy that erupted in that small kitchen in the next instant as Eleanor's foot crossed the threshold.

It was like the stroke of midnight on New Year's Eve, or when the groom kisses the bride at the end of a wedding ceremony, only greater. It was a moment set in time. A moment that I'd never forget. A moment that I couldn't be prouder to be a part of.

The four of us rushed out the door after Eleanor. She was staring up at the stars, wonder filled her face, and she deeply inhaled.

I couldn't help it, tears of happiness freely flowed down my face. Seeing Eleanor bask in happiness was beautiful. It was a sight so simple and yet profound. In that second, I was reminded how the little things could bring so much joy and how we should never take anything for granted because it could be gone in a heartbeat. You can bet that if I hadn't already told Vance how I felt, I'd be running over to his house that instant to do so. I then remembered what Heather had said that afternoon: There's power in forgiveness. It was a Weaver willing to atone for her family's sins, willing to do whatever it took to break Eleanor free. Elizabeth's heart-felt apology and Eleanor's acceptance broke the curse. I was sure that was it.

"Eleanor? Is that you?" Percy was floating down the Enchanted Trail with a fall bouquet of flowers.

"I'm free Percy! Free!" Eleanor giggled as she twirled in the tavern's small courtyard. It was a testament to how weird it can be living in Silverlake that nobody gave the twirling ghost a second glance.

Percy was by Eleanor's side in an instant. His smile was as grand as hers.

"Thank you, Percy. If you hadn't visited me, then Angelica never would have solved it. I owe my happiness to you." Eleanor leaned in and gave Percy a kiss on the cheek.

Percy stammered. I had never seen the poltergeist so flustered in all of my life. I smiled at the scene.

Gone was the sweet ghost with the sad eyes. In her place was a woman filled with joy. If I didn't know any better, I'd swear Eleanor was still alive. "There's so much I want to see. Places I've dreamed of going."

"Where are you going to start?" Bonnie asked

from the doorway. Her arms were folded casually under her chest. Craig stood at her side with his arm draped over her shoulders.

"You know, I think I'd like to start with a tour of Silverlake." Eleanor turned to Percy, "Will you do the honors?"

Percy offered Eleanor his elbow, which she readily slipped her hand through. "I'd be honored. Shall we?"

And like that, the two set off for a nighttime stroll.

I was ready to thank Elizabeth and call Vance to share the excitement of the night when I felt a swift tug at the end of my ponytail. The movement caught me off guard, and I stumbled backward.

"Percy!"

The unseen poltergeist laughed from somewhere unseen before bending close and whispering in my ear, "Thank you, Jelly."

I smiled. "You're welcome, Percy. Glad you're back."

UP NEXT: Untimely Departure.
Book 4 in the *Mystic Inn Mysteries* Series

https://books2read.com/u/3LwRND

Stephanie Damore Complete Works

Mystic Inn Mysteries
Witchy Reservations
Eerie Check In
Spooked Solid
Untimely Departure
Midnight at Mystic Inn

SPIRITED SWEETS MYSTERIES
Bittersweet Betrayal
Decadent Demise
Red Velvet Revenge
Sugared Suspect

.   .   .

WITCH IN TIME
Better Witch Next Time
Play for Time

BEAUTY SECRETS SERIES
Makeup & Murder
Kiss & Makeup
Eyeliner & Alibis
Pedicures & Prejudice
Beauty & Bloodshed
Charm & Deception

A DROP DEAD *Famous Cozy Mystery*
Mourning After

SPIRITED SWEETS MYSTERIES

My name's Claire London and I see dead people.

Just don't tell anyone else or they'll think I'm crazy.

Er...I mean crazier.

My life was beautifully simple.

And then my husband died.

Bit of a shock when his ghost popped up.

Now there are other ghosts who need my help. I'll do whatever it takes to get them up to the Pearly Gates... and out of my bakery.

If you love a clean paranormal mystery, heavy on the whodunit, you're going to love these quick reads!

books2read.com/u/braPyE

ABOUT THE AUTHOR

Stephanie Damore is a USA Today bestselling mystery author with a soft spot for magic and romance, too. She loves being on the beach, has a strong affinity for the color pink (especially in diamonds and champagne), and, not to brag, but chocolate and her are in a pretty serious relationship.

Her books are fun and fearless, and feature smart and sassy sleuths. If you love books with a dash of romance and twist of whodunit, you're going to love her work!

For information on new releases and fun giveaways, visit her Facebook group at https://www.facebook.com/stephdamoreauthor/

- facebook.com/stephdamoreauthor
- twitter.com/stephdamore
- instagram.com/steph_damore_author
- bookbub.com/profile/stephanie-damore